MR. PERKINS
TAKES CHARGE

A TALE OF A VERY SUPERIOR CAT

First Published in the UK 2023

Copyright © 2023 by Suzanne Stephenson

ISBN: 978-1-915953-00-1

Mr. Perkins
Takes Charge

A tale of a very superior cat

Written and illustrated by

Suzanne Stephenson

Also by the author

Bearswood End

'Waste' a comic legal novel(coming soon)

Preface

Mr. Perkins takes charge
A tale of a very superior cat

They say that a philosopher is a blind man in a dark room looking for a black cat that isn't there, but they also say that at night all cats are grey. And it is said that if you are your own lawyer, you have a fool for a client. Nothing is said in popular proverbs about lawyers taking advice from a black cat.

Chapter 1

Mr. Perkins moves in

It was rather a warm morning for early May, so the door of *Spong, Salter and Tethering Solicitors* had been left open. Mr. Perkins just walked in. He sat on the mat just by the reception desk and looked up at the Perspex screen with his tail flat on the floor, his black ears sticking up and his bright amber eyes shining.

"Miaow," he said.

At first no-one took any notice.

"Miaow," he said very loudly.

Maureen, the senior receptionist looked down.

"Where did you come from?" she asked. "I've never seen you before."

"Miaow," he said again.

"Do you think he is hungry?" asked Cora the trainee receptionist.

"He might be," said Maureen who had a soft spot for cats and had two at home.

"Miaow," said Mr. Perkins agreeing.

"He is quite a big cat," said Cora, "but that black coat is a bit dusty so maybe he's fallen on hard times."

"Could be a stray," said Maureen. "There is no collar. I've got some cat treats in my bag for my two and I can get him a little milk from the kitchen although milk is not usually the best thing for cats."

"Miaow," said Mr. Perkins agreeing with her proposal.

She fetched an old saucer and some milk and shook out a handful of cat treats next to it. Mr. Perkins sniffed these offerings and then carefully consumed them. Afterwards he had a little wash and a stretch. Then he looked about the reception area. It was not particularly busy as yet. Most of the chairs had straight backs and even though they had smart blue upholstery they were not intended for relaxation. There was one old leather armchair in a corner with a high back and leather upholstery. Mr. Perkins settled himself down on it for a snooze. As clients came in for their appointments they were lulled by contented purring.

Maureen sent Cora to enquire of neighbouring businesses about the occupant of the armchair, but no-one knew anything about him.

"I wonder what his name is," said Maureen. Mr. Perkins gave her a hard stare with his golden eyes. She tried Tom, Tiddles and Blackie to name but a few. Mr. Perkins continued to purr despite her failure to identify his name. Cora went and stroked him.

"He purrs a lot," said Cora. "Perhaps it's Purr… kins. Do you get it?" she said laughing. Mr. Perkins jumped up immediately and rubbed himself against her.

"Are you Mr. Perkins, you purry pussy?" said Maureen coming over smiling. There was of course a look of immediate recognition on Mr. Perkins' face, an expression which showed that he wondered when they would get there.

Mr. Perkins spent the day in reception and when Maureen and Cora left to go home, he followed them outside with some reluctance. Next morning Maureen brought some dry cat food with her on the off chance he would be there. Sure enough he was on the doorstep waiting. He had some food and settled himself in the armchair and purred. He remained there for the day. This pattern continued for the week. When it got to Friday Maureen expressed concern to Cora.

"What is going to happen for the weekend?" she mused. "I can't just take him home with me. Someone might be looking for him... and I don't know if my two would accept him."

"I could not take home a cat either," said Cora. "Dad is allergic."

In the end Maureen got a large cardboard box and took it around to the side entrance of the firm where there was a porch, where parcels were sometimes left. She turned the box on its side and put some newspaper in it to pad it out. She took a scarf from her handbag and laid it across the newspaper. "Just an old thing I don't need anymore," she muttered. Then she put a bowl of water and a large dish of dry cat food next to it. At five o'clock she picked up Mr. Perkins and carried him around to the items in the porch. Being a gentleman who would not turn down a lady's attempts to help, Mr. Perkins did not scratch her. He sat in his temporary quarters with a look of disdain which could only be expected for a cat hoping for better things, but did not attempt to move away.

On Monday morning Maureen arrived with another box of cat food and a cushion for the make-shift bed in the hopes Mr. Perkins would be there. He was of course waiting outside the office when she arrived very early to unlock the offices and prepare the reception area.

After his meal Mr. Perkins took up his seat in his armchair.

On Tuesday the current senior partner was considering a batch of emails in his oak panelled office when a voice said, "Miaow." Bernard Salter-Smith now bore the responsibility of being the current lead partner. Spong had died years ago, and his own father Leopold Salter had been retired for many years. Titus Tethering aged 83 ought to retire and although he was stone deaf and just about managed to appear two days a week, really he was more of a hindrance than a help.

"Miaow," said Mr. Perkins.

"You must be the cat Maureen is feeding," Bernard said getting up to stroke Mr. Perkins, who gave him a slightly contemptuous look for presumably stating the obvious.

"I like cats although my wife won't let me have one," he said stroking Mr. Perkins who purred loudly.

Bernard's office had a large, panelled leather covered desk and big leather computer chair behind it. There were four leather covered visitors' chairs, a coffee table, three filing cabinets and an antique studded leather office armchair in one corner. Mr. Perkins headed for the antique chair and settled himself down for a snooze. Bernard found the sound of the purring soothing. He had much to think about. Aged fifty-two with receding fair hair, he had a permanently worried look.

First there was the issue of how to persuade old Tethering to retire, then he needed to do something about a nice young couple's house purchase which an assistant had not progressed and then there was an issue about a big financial dispute by a warring couple. These were just a handful of problems but somehow the soothing noise of purring improved his mood.

At one o'clock Bernard was still working when there was a loud, "Miaow," and Mr. Perkins jumped up on his desk and lay just in front of the computer keyboard.

"No, no, no," said Bernard, "keep off the keyboard."

"Miaow," said Mr. Perkins, not moving. Bernard looked at his watch.

"I suppose it is lunchtime," he said.

Mr. Perkins looked up at him and replied, "Miaow."

"Just a minute. I have something you might like," said Bernard approaching a small fridge in the corner of his room. He took out a sandwich box and laid it on the floor.

"My wife keeps giving me tuna salad. There is a lot of tuna in there. I hate tuna salad, so you just help yourself. I might just step out for lunch."

Mr. Perkins jumped down and considered the lunchbox. There was a good deal of tuna sitting on top of a token bit of lettuce, so he started tucking into it.

"Right, I will leave my office door open so you can get out after your lunch. I'm off out."

He saved his work on the computer and pushed the keyboard away from the edge of the desk and headed for the corridor. He bumped into his cheerful red-faced partner Graham Walden who asked if he wanted to pop to the pub for lunch. When Bernard agreed Graham Walden looked surprised.

"Good heavens, that's the first time you said, 'yes' in three years."

The two men strolled around the corner to the *Dog and Duck*. Graham Walden downed a couple of pints and polished off a large plate of 'all day breakfast' while Bernard found he very much enjoyed his pint of shandy and sausage and bacon sandwich.

Graham said, "I see you have taken to our new pussycat member of staff!"

"Yes, he has a calming influence," said Bernard.

"I am very much in favour of animals, in fact I support a number of animal charities," said Graham. "I didn't think you would like it in the past, but do you think it would be alright if we had a collection box and small poster about the dogs' home in reception and a tin for Cat's Protection, too?"

"Well if the poster is small and the other partners plus Mr. Perkins don't mind I would be in favour," replied Bernard.

"Mr. Perkins?" queried Graham.

"The cat," smiled Bernard.

They strolled back to the office. Mr. Perkins was sitting in reception keeping an eye on things. Bernard felt much better for going out. It had helped him to take a break from his work. He had eaten his lunch properly instead of throwing tuna salad in the bin and stuffing his face with crisps and chocolate biscuits while remaining glued to his screen. He paused as he sat down. He decided on a new approach with the young couple's conveyancing; no, not more emails. First, he would phone them and find out their requirements and issues. Then he would phone the other solicitors and discuss the issues and try to overcome any problems.

The telephone call and discussion were fruitful. Before Bernard went home, he stroked Mr. Perkins. Mr. Perkins looked up at him knowingly.

Soon a pattern developed. Mr. Perkins would be at the front door every day. Maureen would feed him, and he would sit purring in reception for a couple of hours or so. Later in the morning he would take himself upstairs to Bernard's office where he would sit in the armchair in the corner. Around one o'clock he would get up and jump on Bernard's desk and lie in front of the keyboard. He would then be provided with a tuna lunch by Bernard who these days either went to the pub with Graham Walden or went for a brisk walk around the nearby park followed by the purchase of a beef and tomato roll and orange juice from the local sandwich shop. After lunch Mr. Perkins tended to spend his time in reception although now and again, he went for a stroll around the offices. The last person to leave the building, be it Maureen or the cleaner would carry him around to his box and make sure there was dry food in the side porch.

Now and again people would work late in the building. Mr. Perkins would stay until he was escorted outside. Enquiries were made of local cat charities and adverts were put on social media, but no-one claimed Mr. Perkins.

One day there was a partners' meeting after normal office hours in the boardroom on the second floor of the building. Seven of the eight partners of the firm had much to discuss including what they were going to do with the old lean-to conservatory at the back of the offices, facing on to the carpark. The backdoor led into it and a number of hot pipes ran through it from the neighbouring boiler house, but at the moment it was only used for storage of mops and buckets since it was not strictly speaking part of the main building. It was underused and currently looked a bit neglected.

The options for the old conservatory were either demolition or repair. They had this to discuss as well as a plethora of other items. The only partner missing was Titus Tethering who had apparently forgotten the meeting.

As the partners were earnestly considering the firm's finances the door which had been slightly ajar was abruptly pushed open and Mr. Perkins jumped on the boardroom table.

"Miaow," he said loudly before sitting down in the middle of the table.

One of the younger partners, Simon Hart-Worthington said,

"I say. Should we move him or something?"

"No," said Graham Walden, "let him stay. Maybe he should be senior partner?" This provoked amusement around the table. Mr. Perkins looked inscrutable.

They carried on with their meeting and eventually they came to the old conservatory. After a great deal of agonising, it was agreed it would be cheaper to repair it than to demolish it. Graham Walden proposed that a cupboard was built in it to house the mops and also once it was repaired some cheap easy chairs were obtained so that it could be a staff break room.

"Miaow," said Mr. Perkins suddenly and loudly.

"Do you think he is trying to tell us something?" asked Bernard.

"I suppose it might be a good place for him in the winter as he has adopted the place," said Graham jovially. "The side porch could get a bit chilly overnight and at weekends."

"Next you will want a cat-door!" said Simon Hart-Worthington disdainfully. It was not that he didn't like cats. It was more that he had wanted the conservatory demolished and replaced with some bicycle stands.

"What a good idea," said Bernard and Graham together.

"There has to be a new outside door to the conservatory anyway. The door leading into the conservatory is locked and alarmed at night so he still could not get into the main building. It seems much more appropriate than leaving him in the porch. We've got some quotes for the door, so it won't be difficult to ask the builders to amend them to include a cat-flap," continued Graham.

The other partners except Simon liked the idea and voted for it to happen. Simon abstained and Mr. Perkins purred very loudly.

"Right," said Graham, "before we adjourn to the pub, any other business?"

"It's about that cat," said Simon. "We are letting it into the office daily, but how do we know it's healthy... it could have fleas?" Mr. Perkins looked affronted.

Graham said, "Good point. If we are adopting him, we should do the job properly."

"That's not what I meant," said Simon, but no-one was listening.

"I agree, Graham," said Bernard.

Ariana Twycross the main family law partner, chipped into the conversation.

"Some of my nervous mums and dads seem to like him. My cat at home has annual jabs against nasty ailments and she is microchipped, and I put stuff on her neck to prevent fleas. Do you not think we should have him checked out and microchipped? I can take him to my vet. I think he should have a collar too and a proper bed."

Mr. Perkins purred very loudly after the words 'proper bed'.

And so it was building works to the conservatory included a cat-flap in the new door. Also, as well as comfy chairs, a soft igloo cat bed was purchased and some brand-new bowls.

One day Ariana arrived to work with a cat-carrying case. She bent down over Mr. Perkins with her long blonde hair flopping over him slightly. She stroked him and he purred loudly. She spoke,

"At lunchtime today we are going for a little ride and then you will be back here and hopefully all the better for it."

Surprisingly, Mr. Perkins was most co-operative getting into the cat carrying case at lunchtime. Fortunately, it only took ten minutes in Ariana's car to reach the vets since Mr. Perkins miaowed loudly indicating his displeasure at the journey. He was not very keen at getting out of the cat-carrying case and spat and hissed at the vet when he was injected and microchipped. Once he was back at the office he dashed upstairs to Bernard's room.

"I know what you want," said Bernard. "Tuna."

"Miaow," agreed Mr. Perkins and made a dive for Bernard's lunchbox. After lunch he sat for a while in the armchair in the corner of the room purring.

Mr. Perkins soon settled down after his trip to the vets. Soon he had a new routine. No longer was he taken to the back porch at the end of the working day. These days he was merely escorted to the conservatory where he had a bed and comfy chairs, and he could come and go through the cat-flap as he wished. Plenty of food was always left for weekends in his bowls.

Bernard let Mr. Perkins settle down into his routine. Indeed, Bernard also had a week's summer holiday to Greece with his wife and daughter. He arranged for Ariana to give Mr. Perkins some tasty treats while he was away. When he returned to the office with rather a pink face and a clearly, sun burned nose, he immediately gave Mr. Perkins a fuss.

"Nice holiday?" asked Maureen.

"My wife enjoyed it," he replied but it was entirely unclear if he had enjoyed it too.

Then, after several more days he came into the office one morning holding a smart red collar with an engraved disc attached.

"Mr. Perkins, I hope you will wear this so people know you belong here," he said to the purring cat.

"Does the disc have the office details?" said Maureen as she helped Bernard put the collar onto Mr. Perkins.

"On one side it has the firm's name and phone number," replied

Bernard. "On the other side of the disc it says 'Mr. Perkins, cat in charge'."

Mr. Perkins purred very loudly.

After he had had his collar put on him, he went round behind the reception desk and jumped up onto it. He sat bolt upright in the middle of the desk peering out through the Perspex screen and said,

"Miaow." He looked very fine. His black coat looked polished, and his eyes shone.

"Well," said Bernard, "I think we can be sure who is in charge now."

Chapter 2
Bernard

Bernard Salter-Smith used to find being senior partner a heavy burden but still marginally preferred being at the office to being at home. These days he approached the office with a spring in his step. Mr. Perkins would greet him in reception and usually ate his tuna lunch. He enjoyed his trips to the pub which he made with Graham Walden once or twice a week. He liked his lunchtime walks in the park where he would sometimes share his sandwich roll with the ducks. On other occasions he would bring a soup or a hot sausage slice back with him and sit in the conservatory with other members of the firm. There, Mr. Perkins would purr loudly and rub around everyone's legs. Occasionally people would ask after his wife and Bernard would answer politely that she was well.

Rosemary Salter-Smith was not his first wife. The love of his life Dina had sadly died of cancer when their daughter Katy was only three years old. Rosemary had been his secretary and he rather feared their romance had developed when he was on the rebound from tragedy. She had seemed to take a huge interest in the welfare of Katy and himself after his wife's death. She would often appear unannounced to bring around casseroles or hoover his house. Although Katy was at nursery school for a good part of the day and went to a child minder for a couple of hours in the afternoon, Bernard toyed with hiring an au pair, but Rosemary came round on increasing occasions and advised him of possible pitfalls. Bernard did not have siblings. His father had at that time recently retired and his parents had gone to live in a villa in Spain. Bernard did not want to worry them with his sense of loss and isolation, so he came to increasingly rely on Rosemary's help.

Rosemary would make intimate dinners in his house after Katy had gone to bed and stroke his hand and tell him how she understood his loss. She started hinting that if there was some permanence to their relationship, she could be persuaded to move into the family home. It was not long before there was a quiet Registry Office wedding and she moved herself into the house. She did explain that as their relationship had been so short, they would have separate bedrooms initially. Katy was now eleven and had recently started secondary school, but they still slept apart. Bernard was confined to what had been a small spare bedroom while Rosemary took the master bedroom; he consoled himself by filling this room and the room he used as an office with books since Rosemary said they looked untidy in the rest of the house. She also insisted she would need to give up work in order to look after the household although as there was a cleaning lady three times a week and Katy started going to after-school clubs from the age of eight it was unclear what she did all day.

When Katy had been two years old Dina had been adamant that she should have a pet in her life and 'Queenie' the grey kitten had joined the household. When Rosemary moved into the house, she sniffed each time she saw Queenie and claimed she upset her sinuses. She was also very concerned about cat hair since she apparently spent a great deal of time dusting and hoovering despite the services of the cleaning lady. The house could be said to absolutely shine. Katy was not allowed to have a toy out of place. Only her bedroom was truly a place she could enjoy her own things.

Bernard's parents Leopold and Alice came over for the wedding. They did not stay long. It was clear they had not taken to their new daughter-in-law. Their visits to Bernard's family were from then on very brief; often just an excuse to collect Katy for a few days and take her to Spain for a holiday. Katy would come back from visiting her grandparents with a smile on her face but would soon become very subdued when she settled into home life. She was such a quiet child that Bernard worried how she would cope with secondary school.

About two years after he had married Rosemary, Bernard came home one day and found all Queenie's cat food, bowls and cat bed had disappeared and there was no sign of Queenie.

"Have you seen the cat?" he said to Rosemary.

"Run over," she replied.

"How dreadful. I am sure Katy will be upset," he responded.

"It was very quick," replied Rosemary ambiguously.

Bernard did not ask anymore. He did not want to know what had really happened. His heart had sunk.

Rosemary had let it be known there would be no more pets. Life became a grind, yet Bernard had become so used to the status quo with Rosemary he had no impetus to change things. He would take the tuna salad to work and work through lunchtime. When he came home there would be a meal of Rosemary's choosing. The evening would be spent with the television turned to soaps or quiz shows which were

Rosemary's choices. At weekends they would go on shopping trips usually to buy an expensive item of clothing for Rosemary and near her birthday or Christmas to buy her a piece of jewellery. Sometimes Bernard would suggest they go to a museum or stately home. He would only get his way if he could persuade Rosemary that it was for Katy's education. The day would then be spent with Rosemary having pursed lips and sighing.

Now and again, Rosemary would want to buy an item for the house. Bernard would find himself purchasing some garish item while he thought wistfully of the seventeenth century engravings, Dina's small collection of Dresden China and her antique walnut desk which along with other items Rosemary regarded as 'old tat', had been confined to the loft. Just after Dina's death he had stored away Dina's jewellery in the bank for Katy's future. Katy was able to avoid some of these shopping expeditions as she was sent for the weekend to Dina's parents from time to time so that Rosemary could throw dinner parties. Although sometimes Graham Walden and his wife were invited more often the people invited were Rosemary's friends. Bernard was not encouraged to invite his old friends to the house, and he doubted they would want to come.

Trips to the zoo or out into the countryside were very rare and holidays were always chosen by Rosemary who made it clear she did not enjoy visiting Bernard's parents. Leopold and Alice were even discouraged from phoning him by Rosemary, so he took to speaking to them later in the day when he was in the office.

Very recently Leopold had rung him.

"You sound very cheerful," said his father.

"Well I have had lunch at the pub today with Graham," replied Bernard.

"Mind that wife of yours doesn't find out," said his father who then asked, "what's that vibrating sound I can hear? It sounds like purring."

"It's Mr. Perkins," replied Bernard who then proceeded to tell his father the whole story of Mr. Perkins' appearance at the office and how he had then moved into the building.

"Well it sounds like he has done you the world of good," said Leopold. "Make sure that wife of yours gets nowhere near him. I always thought she had Queenie put down."

Bernard reassured his father Rosemary would not get her hands on Mr. Perkins.

Bernard lived two lives these days. He appeared the acquiescent husband with Rosemary but at the office he had become calm, sometimes jovial, and much more his own man. He wished he could do more for Katy who seemed to find secondary school a struggle.

One lunch time Mr. Perkins reminded him it was time to take a break by as usual laying in front of the keyboard and saying, "Miaow." He was just placing the tuna salad on the floor when there was a commotion from outside his room. He could hear Cora saying,

"You can't just go in there, he may be busy," but the door burst open, and Rosemary strode in saying, "He is my husband, you can't stop me."

Katy hovered in the doorway and Cora appeared to make a hasty retreat.

Rosemary stopped in her tracks when she saw Mr. Perkins eating the tuna salad. She pointed at him.

"What's that?"

Bernard responded, "He is Mr. Perkins, the office cat or as I think he would like to say if he could 'cat in charge'."

Rosemary went a funny grey-green colour which strangely matched her red hair which had been screwed up into a topknot.

"Why is he eating your lunch?" she queried.

"It's his lunch," said Bernard suddenly emboldened. "He likes tuna fish; I am not that keen."

Rosemary seemed to collapse onto a chair. Katy crept into his office smiling at Mr. Perkins.

"I have had enough trouble with your daughter without you causing trouble too. They sent her home for the afternoon," said Rosemary looking furious. "She's been fighting with other children, so she was suspended for the rest of the day."

"That's not true," cried out Katy.

Rosemary and Katy kept interrupting one another but Bernard was able to piece together the series of events. It appeared that older children had been bullying Katy. She had been allowed to stay in the biology room over the break period to look after the school hamsters and goldfish, as a privilege due to good marks in the subject. She had a large plastic jug of water in her possession which was to top up the goldfish tank. Two of these older girls had entered flashing a cigarette lighter threatening to torch the hamsters' cage, while the biology teacher had gone to fetch a coffee. As they approached the hamsters' cage showing a naked flame which could have ignited the sawdust if they had intended to do more than torment Katy, Katy had instinctively chucked the entire jug of water at them rather than call for help. The biology teacher had just re-entered the room and saw the whole event.

The headmistress had taken the decision to suspend the two girls immediately. However, given that it could have been argued that Katy had overreacted she informally had sent Katy home for the afternoon but made it clear Katy could return tomorrow morning.

"Well, done," said Bernard to Katy. "It is right to stand up to bullies."

Mr. Perkins purred with approval.

"May I stroke him?" asked Katy.

"Of course," replied Bernard.

Rosemary was still seething and issued forth a diatribe against cats and hamsters and pets in general.

"He will have to go," she said pointing at Mr. Perkins who started hissing at her.

"It is not up to you," said Bernard. "The partners have decided he lives here."

"I am the senior partner's wife, and you will do as I say," said Rosemary.

Mr. Perkins jumped onto the middle of Bernard's desk and looking Bernard in the eye he said,

"Miaow."

Somehow Bernard knew it was time to stand up to Rosemary.

Bernard spoke,

"Unlike our marriage, Rosemary, the firm has a true partnership where the partners make decisions together and more than one voice prevails. The decision of the partners was to adopt Mr. Perkins."

"What do you mean?" said Rosemary sounding livid. "I gave up my job to take care of Katy and you."

"You were my secretary," said Bernard, "not a partner of the firm. I admit we have a very clean and tidy house, but everything is as you want things. There is no thought to what I want."

"Well what do you want if it's not a clean and tidy house?" said Rosemary in shrill tones.

"I want... I want..." said Bernard also turning up the volume, "I want a home not just a clean house. I want to feel I can relax there, read books, have friends and relations round. I want Katy to have pets if she wants them… to feel she can have friends round or her grandparents to visit. And," he drew in breath, "I don't want tuna salad for lunch."

"You want to fill the house with dirty smelly pets and untidy books?"

"Yes," responded Bernard standing his ground. "I want a home not a show-house."

"I have never been spoken to like this," said Rosemary. "And to think all I have done for Katy and yourself. Seven years of my life I have given you, only to find I am so unappreciated, and you would rather give preference to that cat… Well either the cat goes, or I shall be leaving you."

"Mr. Perkins is not going anywhere," said Bernard, with Mr. Perkins adding a background, "Miaow."

Rosemary said, "We'll see about that," and made to grab him from the desk. There was a hiss and a yowl and a tussle and then a yelp from Rosemary and Mr. Perkins jumped off the desk and made for his armchair.

"He has attacked me," said Rosemary. "Look - toothmarks on my hand and a scratch to my arm. He is vicious."

There was a minute mark to her hand and a large scratch down her arm.

"I didn't see Mr. Perkins do anything, did you, Katy?" said Bernard with a wry smile.

"No. I didn't see anything, Dad," said Katy, and then with inventiveness she added, "I think Rosemary must have scratched her arm in the garden this morning."

Mr. Perkins sat in the chair and fixed Rosemary with a hard stare while emitting a low growling type noise.

Rosemary said,

"I am not staying here a minute longer and indeed I shall be planning on packing when I get home."

Then she flounced out leaving Bernard and Katy speechless for a minute. Mr. Perkins stopped growling and went to each of them in turn, rubbing against them and purring loudly.

"You were very brave, Dad, standing up to her. I never thought you would," said Katy.

"If you can stand up to bullies it is time I did too!" responded Bernard.

"Do you think she'll go?" asked Katy.

"I rather hope she does," said her father.

"What if she takes lots of stuff from the house?" asked Katy.

"So what if she does?" said Bernard. "We can manage."

There was a knock at the door of his room. It was Maureen.

"Excuse me, is everything okay? Mrs. Salter-Smith just ran out of the office shouting about a vicious cat attack. Also, your two o'clock appointment has arrived."

"We are all fine in here," said Bernard while Katy smiled, and Mr. Perkins blinked enigmatically. "I don't know what she was talking about. However, Katy has the afternoon off school so she will stay here and talk to Mr. Perkins while I see the clients in the boardroom."

Later in the afternoon Maureen arranged for Katy to have a chocolate drink and for Mr. Perkins to have a saucer of milk in the conservatory rest room. There was a lot of purring.

"He's made such a difference to the office since he adopted the firm," said Maureen.

Katy smiled shyly. "I think I will visit him lots," she said.

After Bernard had finished work, to Katy's surprise, he did not take them straight home.

"I am taking you out to supper because I am not sure what we'll find at home."

The *Dog and Duck* had a family dining room which started serving meals to families from five-thirty, so he treated them both to pasta and salad followed by ice-cream sundaes. When they got home about quarter past seven a van had just pulled out of the driveway.

"That was Uncle Wayne," said Katy referring to Rosemary's brother.

When they got in the house it was plain Rosemary had gone. All her clothes and jewellery had gone. The Hi-fi system had gone. The televisions from the master bedroom and kitchen had gone. The television in the living room was still there but there were some scuff marks near the wall mountings, so Bernard suspected Rosemary and Wayne had difficulty taking it off the wall. Rosemary's laptop had gone as had the printer from Bernard's office but fortunately his desktop was unscathed. Several small kitchen appliances had disappeared as had a large orange vase from the hall which Bernard had always considered hideous. Some modern reproduction pictures had disappeared from the walls and strangely the orange scatter cushions which had graced the mauve settees had gone as well.

"It's a pity she didn't take the settees too," said Bernard. "I never liked them. It's a bit mean she took the kettle and toaster, but I am sure we can manage. I will have the locks changed in the morning."

"It's just you and me now, Dad," said Katy.

"I am sure we shall manage," said Bernard. "And I think we should get some pets, too."

Katy smiled. "I would like that. I don't suppose we can have Mr. Perkins?"

"I think he has settled into the office so it might not be fair to move him. But how about a house rabbit or some guinea pigs to start? Maybe in a while a cat or a dog as well, when things have settled down."

Katy was very enthusiastic.

Next day when Bernard was at the office, he spoke to Mr. Perkins seriously as if he was speaking to a person.

"What have you done to my life, friend? Did you intend to turn things upside down? Mind you, it was no bad thing."

Mr. Perkins just purred, and Bernard served him some gourmet cat food on a saucer. Bernard knew everything would turn out fine.

MiaoW !

Chapter 3

Graham and David

Over the next few weeks Bernard and Katy settled down to life without Rosemary. Katy became the owner of Bennybuns a grey and white fluffy rabbit and Snuffleface a brown and white guinea pig. She visited Mr. Perkins at least weekly. By agreement, Bernard let Uncle Wayne take more of the hideous furniture from the house. He stopped bringing tuna salad to work but brought Mr. Perkins some tasty cat food or a slice of chicken each day. Katy's schoolwork improved and despite having a messy divorce Bernard approached his life and his work with much more enthusiasm.

Mr. Perkins would from time to time visit other members of staff these days. One day he happened to march into Graham Walden's room.

"Miaow," he announced himself.

Graham Walden was eating a large ham and cheese roll. He broke off a piece of ham and offered it to the cat.

"Hello, Mr. Perkins, have you come to sort me out?"

"Miaow," came the response.

Graham had been going to have a crafty nip of whisky from the bottle he hid in his desk drawer. It wasn't that it was a particularly fine whisky, but it was accessible. He also had a hidden hip flask in his briefcase and another bottle in his filing cabinet in the 'x' section. If he was going to be honest with himself, he had a bit of a problem with alcohol. At home he thought he was more of a connoisseur. He enjoyed his clarets and single malts but there was so much else to engross him his consumption was quite modest. There were Buddy and Buster his Labradors to walk, golf to be played at his local club and his wife Mary's charities to support. She was on the Board of Trustees of the local dog and cat rescue charities not to mention having a part-time role for a national pet charity, fund-raising. Here at the office for reasons he could not fathom he would have crafty nips throughout the working day. He knew he should stop but he just had not got round to it.

Mr. Perkins rubbed at his legs, and he found himself saying,

"I will just see if Maureen has any milk for you."

He phoned down to reception.

"Sorry to bother you, but is there any chance of a saucer of milk for Mr. Perkins?"

"Yes of course," came the response. "And would you like a coffee?"

Soon Graham Walden found himself sipping coffee while Mr. Perkins lapped up his milk. Loud purring followed.

"I am just going to check the cricket scores, Mr. Perkins," he said to the cat who was gazing at him enigmatically. He looked at his computer screen and started to read them out.

"This Test Match isn't going so well," said Graham.

"Miaow," said Mr. Perkins to Graham who was starting to open the drawer to get out the hipflask. "Miaow," said Mr. Perkins again and pushed it shut with his nose.

"That's stopped me," laughed Graham.

The phone rang. It was one of the other partners.

"Yes, of course, send him now," he said.

"We have to try and sort out the new trainee," he said to Mr. Perkins who of course replied,

"Miaow."

Graham was a man of seemingly endless patience and good humour; hence he had been put in charge of staff welfare and training issues. He sighed at the thought of trying to sort out young David Dines who had been with the firm four months. It was hard to know where to start with him. He wanted to open the desk drawer or reach for his hip flask but there was a risk he might be seen by young David.

David came with impeccable exam results and references and performed well at interview. However, some of the staff had taken to calling him 'Dim David' or 'Davy Dimbo' behind his back. Graham would have the unenviable job of disciplining any name calling and sorting out young David who had hardly made life easy for himself. First there was the matter of the terrible tight blue suit he had taken to wearing to work which made him look as if he had just left a cheap nightclub. Then his long greasy mousy hair needed washing and cutting or at the least tying back. It surely can't have helped his spots.

David's timekeeping was poor. He was always late in the mornings, sometimes charging through the door munching a sandwich and clutching a takeaway coffee, which on two occasions he had spilled in reception. Once he was late because he had mislaid his bus season ticket due to leaving it in his suit trousers when they went to the wash. For someone with a good law degree it was incredible that he found it so difficult to draft a letter. When called upon to interview clients for purposes of preparing a statement it was quite 'hit and miss' what might happen.

The first time he had been asked to interview clients in those circumstances he had run off to the gents' and was sick. Two more occasions followed when he stammered to such an extent the clients complained they found him difficult to understand. He had been sent once to the Crown Court to make notes about a trial. He got lost on the way, but to give him his due his notes were of good quality. Graham had the unenviable job of sorting out Davy Dines without upsetting him.

There was a timid knock at Graham's door. Mr. Perkins said, "Miaow," and Graham said, "Come in."

Davy gulped and sidled into the room. He looked like the rabbit caught in the headlights of a car. Davy had no idea why the world of work terrified him. At school he had always been top of the class. His mother had said it was because he studied so hard, even in the holidays. She therefore said that he was excused getting a holiday job. At university he excelled at his studies and was the leading light of the university debating society. His mother encouraged him to rest in the holiday when he was not studying. He had held down two part-time jobs in his university holidays. One was cataloguing history books for the local historical society and the other was preparing inventories of stationery supplies for a local stationery wholesaler. In neither case did he have much to do with people and they certainly did not stretch him intellectually. He was involved in his local church and helped prepare the church for Sunday service and tidy it afterwards. Sometimes he even read a lesson at church with no difficulty.

His parents lived apart although they were not divorced. Jack Dines spent a lot of his time away anyway since he was an oilrig engineer. When he saw his son, he always seemed to make jibes. Davy did not think he could ever satisfy his father about anything. His dad had laughed when he started studying.

"You, a lawyer. No, don't make me laugh," said Jack.

When Davy got a good degree and studied for his professional exams Jack said, "No they must have got the wrong lad, muddled you with someone else." He had been similar in Davy's schooldays even though Davy was consistently having good results.

By contrast Mrs. Dines was overprotective and interfering. She chose all Davy's clothes, expressed her ideas strongly about his hobbies and seemed very discouraging to any friends or girlfriends he tried to bring home to the extent that Davy had no close friends.

"Sit down, Dave," said Graham amiably. Dave did as he was bid. Mr. Perkins rubbed around his legs and jumped on his knee.

"Now then," Graham continued, "it's time to review your progress."

Davy nodded nervously.

"It's very difficult joining the world of work if you are not used to it. Let's start with what your aspirations are," continued Graham.

"I really want to be a solicitor like you, sir," said Davy.

"Graham will do." Graham indeed continued. "Do you think you look the part of an aspiring solicitor?"

"You mean my clothes?" said Davy who had suspected his mother's taste was not the best and that getting something as she put it 'modern and trendy' did him no favours at all. Mr. Perkins took the opportunity to dig his claws into Davy's lap.

"Ouch," said Davy. "His claws nearly got my... Ouch... you know where."

"I don't think he likes your suit," said Graham laughing. "What happened to the one you wore for the interview?"

"It's in the wardrobe. Mum bought me this one. She said I needed something more modern."

"Well, I don't think Mr. Perkins agrees." They both laughed. Graham wondered how he would tell Davy to do something about his hair. He continued,

"You should formulate a style of what you think makes you look the part. It is not your mum who has to come to work. My barber Burt on the High Street makes me neat and tidy. Why don't you go and see him for a bit of a re-style... say I sent you. And he'll no doubt treat you kindly."

Mr. Perkins purred. Graham would ask Burt to send most of the bill to him.

"You've spent a little time with a couple of the departments," said Graham. "They all say you seem to have trouble with your nerves."

Davy nodded and Mr. Perkins rubbed against him.

"I guess dealing with real people and real cases is so different than learning legal theory or debating," said Davy.

"People are generally weird," said Graham in jocular tones. "Don't let anyone get to you... I will never understand all of them. Just get on with the job and don't let any of them upset you."

Davy nodded but still looked as white as a sheet.

"Look," Graham found himself saying, "why don't you shadow me for a couple of weeks? I might give you the odd job to do but I won't bite if you get things wrong."

"Miaow!" said Mr. Perkins.

Davy started smiling at Mr. Perkins and stroked him.

"He's a great cat," he said.

Mr. Perkins' ears went up and he purred even louder.

"Yes," said Graham. "Some of the clients enjoy his presence too, so if he wants to join you in any interviews do let him. He knows when people are allergic to cats somehow and will give them a wide berth."

"Miaow," said Mr. Perkins apparently agreeing.

Davy already felt better. Graham went on.

"This afternoon I am going to ask you to do a small task for me. Mr. Perkins' presence has brought to the fore that the firm does not have a policy about how to help people onto the premises with Guide dogs or other companion animals. I am going to give you the office manual to read. Then I want you to draft something about Guide dogs and companion animals. You might also want to look at the firm's standard pro forma letters; do we need a client care letter for people with disabilities, about their rights etc.? You can do your reading in the staff restroom. Should be nice and quiet. You can even take a laptop in there. Is that okay?"

Davy said,

"I didn't know we had proforma letters." Graham thought that he was getting somewhere with the lad; it sounded like no-one had pointed these out to Davy. "I would be really pleased to look at them and thank you for trusting me with these jobs."

"Miaow," said Mr. Perkins in agreement.

Davy took the office manual to the staff restroom.

Graham reached for the bottom drawer but once again Mr. Perkins pushed it in with his nose. He tried opening the filing cabinet with the 'x' section but yet again Mr. Perkins pushed it in with his nose. Finally, he tried to get his hip flask from his briefcase, but the cat sat on it and hissed at him when he tried to move him off it.

"I give up!" said Graham. "You've won! Shall we go instead to the kitchen, and I'll get a cup of tea and we'll find you something tasty, I'm sure?"

Mr. Perkins climbed off the briefcase and purred loudly.

They headed to the kitchen.

Over the next few weeks while Mr. Perkins would spend some time in reception and always called in on Bernard, he spent a considerable amount of time with Graham and Davy. These days Davy had given up on the tight 'modern' suit purchased by his mother. He wore the suit he had used at interview and his hair had been trimmed and was neatly tied back. One day he showed up in a smart pinstripe suit.

"My," said Maureen, at reception, "don't you look smart."

"Thank you," said Davy blushing.

Mr. Perkins purred and had an odd knowing look.

"He likes it," said Cora.

"It was the strangest thing," said Davy who felt confident enough to tell his story. "Last Friday Mr. Perkins followed me out of the office when I left to go home. It was about 4.30 and Mr. Walden said I could go early. I was really worried because the cat followed me round the corner to the High Street. I kept saying 'Go home. Go back to the office' but he wouldn't leave my side. Eventually I was bending to pick him up and he ducked away from me and headed a few feet into a shop doorway where he made the loudest 'Miaow' I have ever heard. Well, it was a charity shop and there in the window was this suit! It was as if Mr. Perkins knew.

"I managed to get him under my arm and headed inside. I asked about the suit, and it was my size, and nearly new and Mr. Perkins purred very loudly. The lady laughed when I bought it while still holding Mr. Perkins under my arm! Of course, I brought him straight back afterwards and he just settled down in one of his usual spots!"

"Ah, that accounts for why you came back into the office with Mr. Perkins at the end of Friday," said Maureen. "Clever cat!"

Graham was also most amused to hear the story and was further pleased with Davy's increasing confidence. He had decided to send Davy when his client Mrs. Truegold met her barrister Mr. Fortescue for a preliminary conference in preparation for a maintenance hearing against her ex-husband. Graham could see Davy had made an effort about his appearance. He told Davy of his requirements and added,

"Mr. Perkins and I have every confidence in you!"

Mr. Perkins purred.

"I think he is somehow lucky!" said Davy. "He pointed out my suit."

Mr. Perkins looked suitably enigmatic.

Davy went to the conference. He didn't get lost. He didn't suffer an attack of nerves. He made a careful note of Mr. Fortescue's advice and reassured Mrs. Truegold that he would give a full report to Graham. It all went like clockwork.

Meanwhile Graham was carefully going over a draft lease for Mr. Ali. Mr. Ali was a well-established client who was wishing to move his restaurant to larger premises. It was known locally for its south Indian cuisine. The new location was to be in the middle of the High Street in the premises of what had been an unsuccessful Greek restaurant which had only lasted about two years. Before the Greek restaurant the premises had been a successful English steakhouse for about ten years before the chain went bust. The freeholder was a shark, so Graham felt it was important to go through the lease with a fine toothcomb. He spent two hours sorting out the finer points but eventually found himself reaching for the bottom drawer.

"Miaow," said Mr. Perkins and pushed it shut with his nose. Then he jumped onto Graham's desk. Graham had left the morning paper on the side of his desk. The draft lease was in the middle of the desk. Mr. Perkins sat himself down on the draft lease and flicked the morning paper off the desk with his nose. It fell on the floor and fell open on the crossword page at Graham's feet.

"Heavens," said Graham, "I haven't done the crossword for quite a while. Are you trying to tell me it's lunchtime and we should look for something nice to eat, and maybe I should do the crossword?"

Mr. Perkins looked suitably inscrutable.

Graham found himself doing the crossword over his lunch. Apart from his pub lunches his consumption of alcohol in the office melted away. One evening he found himself removing the hip flask from his briefcase and pouring the contents away. The flask itself was shoved to the back of a cupboard way out of sight. The next day, with Mr. Perkins looking on he removed the bottles of whisky from his drawer and the filing cabinet and placed them in the sideboard in the boardroom, which had a selection of odd bottles that came out on special occasions.

One day his wife Mary called in at the offices to sort out the collection boxes and a small display for the local animal charities which the partners had agreed could be placed there. Mr. Perkins had been washing himself while sitting on the chair in the corner of reception, but he paused grooming and came up to Mary and rubbed around her legs and purred.

"So you are the famous Mr. Perkins," she said smiling. "Are you as clever as they say?"

"Very clever," said Graham and Davy Dines together as they both came into reception. Introductions followed between Davy and Mary Walden.

Mr. Perkins just said, "Miaow" but otherwise looked inscrutable.

Flora

Chapter 4

Simon Hart-Worthington

S imon had a first at Oxford and a Master's degree from Harvard University; he was fit, smart and good looking and apparently had no relationships. He was the firm's expert in Commercial Litigation and Tax Law. Corporate clients in the surrounding counties flocked to the firm because of his expertise. From time to time 'head-hunters' from City firms tried to lure him away without success. Simon preferred the relative stability of a provincial firm than the possibility of joining a 'hire and fire' outfit in the City for a huge salary. He had a riverside mews house in an expensive development the other side of town with views onto the local river. In the garages near the development, he had a *Porsche* car which he rarely used. He travelled to and from work by bicycle which was the most up to date model for serious hobby cyclists.

His house was furnished in a Spartan way. It was not that he did not want more in his home; more that he had not seen the need to put more into his home. There was a room devoted to fitness equipment, a small room was set up as a 'home office', there was a sitting-dining area which opened out onto a patio, his bedroom, the kitchen, the bathroom and a rarely used spare bedroom. A local cleaning company, *Brilliant Maids* came once a week. The kitchen was full of the latest appliances which he rarely used, and the sitting area and dining area was furnished with modern angular furniture and was devoid of character.

He was a leading light at the local fitness gym and also of the over thirties' group of the local cycling club. He rarely saw his family who lived about one hundred miles away. Sometimes he felt a pang of regret, a feeling that there was something missing. He recalled growing up in a sprawling chaotic house full of his brothers and sisters and family dogs. His parents ran a large farm and he smiled when he remembered playing with the Labradors and Cocker Spaniels who usually ended up lying in front of the Aga. He would go home twice a year, once at Christmas and for a weekend mid-summer. His older brother and his wife and children now lived at the farm so his brother could help their elderly parents run it. His younger brother had become an accountant and was with a practice in the town nearest the farm where he lived with his wife and young baby. His older sister was head of the Geography Department at the local high school in the same town and now engaged to be married. His youngest sister had just qualified as a doctor. She was joining an overseas charity for a year but had said she then wanted to work nearer to home on her return.

He had never been a cat person although he didn't dislike them. He always preferred dogs. He was therefore slightly non-plussed when Mr. Perkins began to visit him on his constitutional around the offices.

These days after Maureen had given him breakfast and he had enjoyed a little snooze in reception Mr. Perkins would take his constitutional around the building and during his walk inspect his people. He would of course call on Bernard who would have been disappointed if he did not visit. He called on Graham and Davy Dines if they were in the building. Graham laughed inwardly that the cat was checking up on him. Davy always made time to stroke his head if he was there and he would still sometimes sit in on Davy's interviews with clients. He visited Ariana Twycross during his rounds and now he would sit in Simon's room often looking at him inscrutably.

Initially Simon and Mr. Perkins would sit silently together. If Simon was working at the computer, he would feel the hairs on the back of his neck tingle. He would turn around and find Mr. Perkins giving him a hard stare.

"What do you want, cat? I've nothing to give you," said Simon and Mr. Perkins would just stare at him in a knowing way.

The visits to Bernard, Graham and Davy were often fairly short and the visits to Simon increased in length. Simon had a sports' bag and would change into his cycling attire at lunchtime and go for a 30-minute ride around the local park. Mr. Perkins had taken to curling up on Simon's sports' bag which meant that each lunchtime Simon had to lift him off the bag. He mentioned this to Maureen when she brought him a cup of tea one afternoon when he was particularly snowed under with work.

"Does he complain at you when you try to move him or try to bite or scratch you?" asked Maureen.

"No, he just gives me one of his stares," said Simon tolerating her questions but not really knowing where they were going.

"That is unusual," said Maureen. At that moment Mr. Perkins entered the room.

"Perhaps he is trying to tell you something," said Maureen.

"Miaow, miaow," said Mr. Perkins by way of agreement. Simon still did not understand.

One day he plonked his sports' bag down and left the zipper slightly open in the hopes it might deter Mr. Perkins. However, Mr. Perkins just made himself comfortable on the heap of clothes inside the bag. Around one o'clock Simon was going to change into his cycling gear when he heard a horrible noise emanating from Mr. Perkins who was now sitting up with his back arched.

"E-guh, e-guh, e-guh," went Mr. Perkins and sicked up a large fur-ball and a bit of his breakfast on Simon's sports' clothes.

"Oh no, no no… horrid cat," yelled out Simon.

Bernard was walking along the corridor and poked his head into Simon's office.

"Look what that wretched cat has done," said Simon.

"Poor pussy," said Bernard. "Was it a nasty fur-ball?" He stroked Mr. Perkins who had got off the bag and was rubbing round his legs. Simon glowered at Mr. Perkins.

"Whatever am I going to do? I can't go cycling now. All my stuff will need to be washed," moaned Simon.

"Why don't you go for a brisk walk around the park? I often go there," said Bernard. "Sorry I can't join you today but I'm off to an 'Open Day' at Katy's school."

Mr. Perkins said, "Miaow," in apparent agreement with the suggestion.

Simon grumpily took up the idea.

Joe Gordon wearily walked with his stick around the duck pond. After years of having the Army to be a supportive family, civvy street felt strange. It wasn't an IED in Afghanistan which had invalided him out of the Army but a car accident taking him to a training exercise in the Brecon Beacons. He knew he had done well to hold down a job three days a week at Customer Services at the local supermarket and to find the little flat in his hometown close to his mother and sister. Nonetheless he felt downhearted. The physiotherapist said he needed to walk regularly to strengthen his muscles.

"Have a dog," she suggested breezily, but he was not allowed pets in his flat.

His counsellor also suggested that if he was able, a companion animal might be a good idea.

He had nodded and not discussed his deep disappointment that added to his other problems he could not have a pet. So, most days when it was fine, and he was free from work he would head to the duck pond with a pocket full of bread crusts. He would walk around the pond and then sit on a bench and enjoy the quacking and squabbling on the duck pond. It was a peaceful spot away from the children's play area which was the other side of the park.

Simon had initially entered the park feeling very resentful towards Mr. Perkins. After a short time, he became aware of the sound of birdsong and admired the lustrous plant life and flowers. He had not been to this park before despite working so close to it for a considerable period, and against his instincts was beginning to enjoy his walk. He felt somewhat grudgingly that maybe Mr. Perkins had done him a favour. He broke into a jog.

As Simon came around a bend in the path near the duck pond he found himself knocking into a figure with a stick. Fortunately, Joe did not fall over but he seemed to be teetering on the brink. Simon pulled him up and said,

"I really am so sorry. Entirely my fault. Let me help you to the bench just there."

Joe mumbled that he was alright, but Simon gently guided him to the bench.

"Phew," said Simon. "Well I needed to sit down anyway."

They sat together for a few minutes in embarrassed silence then Simon said,

"It's the first time I have come here. It really is a very pleasant spot."

"Yes, it is," said Joe smiling. "I come here frequently to try to get my strength back."

The two men got into a nervous conversation and Joe explained about his accident and how he had been in the Army. Simon explained that he usually went cycling in his lunch hour but that he had come to the park today for a change. They chatted for a while. Eventually Simon said,

"Look I think I will come to the park tomorrow lunchtime. Can I buy you a cup of coffee from the park café then as recompense for nearly sending you flying?"

Simon and Joe met the next day. The sports' bag did not come to the office for a while. Before he went out Simon found himself talking to Mr. Perkins who was sitting upright in the middle of the office,

"No sports' bag for you to vomit on today."

"Miaow," responded Mr. Perkins. Simon found himself bending down and scratching Mr. Perkins behind the ears.

"Not such a bad thing that I went to the park," added Simon. Mr. Perkins looked inscrutable and purred.

Although from very different backgrounds Simon and Joe seemed to have struck up a rapport. They talked of their backgrounds and histories. Simon even mentioned Mr. Perkins. They agreed they would have lunch together on Saturday at a nearby Italian place. They regularly met for walks, coffees, and the odd meal. Conversation turned to Mr. Perkins and to animals one day.

"You seem very taken with the office cat," said Joe.

"WELL, HE'S A BIT OF a mystery," said Simon who described Mr. Perkins' sudden appearance one day. "I find myself having taken to him despite the fact I am more of a dog person. I really miss having a dog."

Joe responded,

"I've been advised a dog would do me good both physically and with morale, but I am not allowed to have a dog in my flat. I really do like dogs."

Simon looked thoughtful.

"Well maybe there is a way we could share a dog. I think we should visit the local dog rescue centre together... and work around the problem."

Mary Walden was helping out at the Dog Rescue Centre on Saturday when Simon and Joe called into their rehoming kennels. Simon and Joe travelled separately. Simon made a mental note that the sporty *Porsche* would be no good for having a dog. He had noticed Joe's beaten-up old car in the car park. That had very little room in the back for a dog.

Mary recognised Simon from office functions and smiled and greeted him. He soon introduced her to Joe. He told her a little about the wish to share a dog with Simon. If she had any questions about their relationship, she did not ask them. Her concentration was on the dog and how they would care for him or her. The two men explained the dog would live at Simon's house but as Joe only worked part-time, he would come to the house when he was not working to care for the dog. They would both exercise their doggy pal.

Mary thought carefully and said,

"We have Flora. She is a Labrador Staffie cross. She has been spayed. She is five years old. Originally, she lived with an old lady who sadly died. Then a young woman with five small children took her on but it was just too much. She is house-trained. She might pull a bit on the lead so Joe might need to be careful, but I think she will respond to training. Would you like to meet her?"

Joe positively beamed and both Simon and Joe said, "Yes please."

She was a golden-brown dog who looked more Labrador than Staffie. At first, she seemed nervous and seemed to hold back. After some moments she came timidly forward and licked first Joe's hand, then Simon's hand. Joe and Simon took her for a short walk and petted her, and they then resolved to visit her at least five times over the next ten days before taking her home to Simon's house.

When Simon was next in the office, Mr. Perkins said, "Miaow," to announce himself as he came into Simon's office during his constitutional.

"I'm getting a dog with Joe," said Simon to the cat who replied with a purr. "I think it's all due to you." The purring increased but Mr. Perkins looked enigmatic. "If you hadn't done something revolting to my sports' kit, I would never have gone to the park and met Joe…"

Ariana Twycross was just passing Simon's office and peered into his room.

"Having a chat with the boss?" she laughed.

"He is the boss, isn't he!" laughed Simon in response.

Mr. Perkins gave them both a hard stare before following Ariana back to her room.

Simon realised that in the past he would not have joined in with such levity. He recalled his initial opposition to Mr. Perkins. Now he could not imagine the office without Mr. Perkins. His thoughts then turned to the changes he needed to make to his mews house. He had already ordered a big dog bed, dog food, dog leads and some dog toys, and was even thinking about changing his car. The patio opened out onto a lawned area which stopped at another patio which was a terrace above the river. There was then a flight of steps down to a small landing stage where he kept a rowing boat. He would have some fencing and a gate put up on his riverside terrace. He didn't want Flora to get into difficulties in the river since sometimes there were quite large powerful boats going up and down. He would get some garden furniture too. Joe might like to sit outside with Flora and for that matter so might he.

The ten-day period flew past. The doggy visits were each more successful than the last one. Simon managed to change his car to a smart SUV with plenty of space in the back for a dog and do most of the things on his list. The garden fencing was almost finished, and the contractor would be putting in the final touches tomorrow. The garden furniture would be delivered by the end of that week.

Simon had a spring his step. His world seemed much improved.

Mr. Perkins had made his usual visits and was spending quite some time these days with Ariana Twycross but nonetheless he found time to call in on Simon.

"Miaow," said Mr. Perkins announcing himself.

"Hello, there, pal," said Simon. "Come to check up on me?"

"Miaow," said Mr. Perkins again.

"Joe and I are getting a dog," said Simon. Mr. Perkins purred. "She is coming home on Saturday, the day after tomorrow."

Mr. Perkins went up to him and rubbed around him.

"Okay, okay I need to get on now," laughed Simon.

Mr. Perkins continued his rounds with his tail sticking up like a rudder.

Flora came to live at the riverside mews house. She soon settled down under the care of Simon and Joe. Slowly there were changes in the mews house. As well as doggy bowls and doggy beds a couple of framed photographs of Flora appeared on the walls plus one of Simon's family farm. Some cushions with Labrador designs appeared on the settee and a fluffy warm rug appeared in the middle of the living room floor. A coat stand with doggy leads and coats and human overcoats for dog walking appeared near the patio doors. There were packs of dog food in the kitchen and a dog charity calendar had appeared on the wall. The somewhat clinical house was turning into a home.

After some weeks Bernard was talking to Simon over some coffee in the small office kitchen.

"Mary wants to know how Joe and you are getting on with Flora," he asked.

"She's an absolutely great dog. We've had no trouble. She has learned to walk properly on her lead. She comes when she is called. I could not ask for better…"

Mr. Perkins appeared purring and gave them both a hard stare.

"And how is Joe getting on with the arrangement?" asked Bernard.

Simon cleared his throat.

"Joe is moving in with Flora and I. Much better for all of us."

Bernard knew better than to ask for any further details.

Mr. Perkins just looked enigmatic.

Chapter 5
B u r g l a r s

Bernard and Katy had settled down very well. They really did not miss Rosemary and Katy was able to have a much better relationship with her grandparents. Although Rosemary was making all sorts of financial demands Bernard took the view that even if Katy and himself had to move to a smaller house their lives would be richer in other ways. Katy had her pets Bennybuns and Snuffleface and she would frequently visit Mr. Perkins. Bernard found himself promising Katy a kitten as soon as things settled down. In the meantime, he was developing some new interests. He and Katy signed up as friends of the local zoo and they became frequent visitors to special events and lectures. Katy was awestruck when they were part of a private dusk visit to the zoo. Events such as that encouraged Bernard to revive a dormant hobby of photography.

Katy could not resist dragging her dad to any fund-raising events for the local dogs' home as well. Graham and Mary Walden were delighted to see them at the dogs' home annual cake sale. They chatted over a delicious display of cakes and dogs could be heard barking in the background.

Bernard and Graham still went out for lunch once a week to the local pub. On other occasions they shared a brisk walk together. Bernard could not resist saying to Mary,

"I don't know what it is, but I have noticed how fit Graham looks these days."

Mary laughed and Graham retorted,

"Could say the same about you, Bernard! I call it the Perkins' effect."

They all agreed that Mr. Perkins had a beneficial effect on most people and Katy said she would bring him some tuna next time she went into the office because she knew how much he enjoyed it.

Various familiar figures drifted into the cake sale. Simon and Joe arrived with Flora who wagged her tail vigorously and was plied with dog treats.

"I am glad you have a good turn-out," said Joe. "Dogs like Flora deserve to have good lives. I have been walking with her daily and I am sure I won't need a stick for long."

"And cats too," said Katy joining in the conversation. "Like Mr. Perkins."

"Indeed," said Bernard. "Like Mr. Perkins. I wonder what he is doing right now?"

As it was Saturday there had not been much activity in the office. Davy Dines had come in briefly and taken a statement from a witness. He was then going to a function run by the local Trainee Lawyers' Group which he had recently joined. They were spending the afternoon ten-pin bowling and afterwards going out for a pizza. Ariana Twycross also came into the office. She interviewed a grandmother, and her client, the fifteen-year-old granddaughter. As Ariana was leaving, the firm's maintenance man Fred Boggis arrived.

Ariana politely reminded Fred of the alarm codes and to lock up properly when he left.

Mr. Perkins had slept late as the office was quiet and he was confined to the conservatory. He had plenty of dry kibble to eat. Ariana did tiptoe in and leave him a saucer of *Empress delicate morsels* gourmet cat food. When he woke up, he sniffed this saucer carefully and then made it disappear in seconds. He did a lot of grooming and washing next. His hackles could be seen to rise, and his ears went up when Fred Boggis came into the near empty offices and started banging about on the ground floor. Nonetheless Mr. Perkins slipped out through the cat-door for a while and patrolled the outer edges of the car park and the ventilation grills to the cellars. Soon he returned with a fat mouse which he proceeded to carefully dismember in the conservatory. After his mouse Mr. Perkins climbed up onto some shelving which housed a few legal magazines but was also a place where he sometimes could be found having a nap.

Fred had made it plain on previous occasions he did not like Mr. Perkins one bit, so it was a good thing Fred was working in the main building and Mr. Perkins was eating his mouse and then snoozing in the conservatory.

When Ariana came to the building that day Fred Boggis said,

"I hate that bloody moggy, keep it away from me, it always looks at me as if it knows summit."

Ariana protested that Mr. Perkins had done nothing but good for the firm. Fred Boggis continued to grumble,

"He gives me the evils… the way he looks at me."

Indeed, when today's visitors to Ariana had first come to the firm it was Mr. Perkins who had calmed them down. Fifteen-year-old Jade was subject to proceedings before the Family Court and Ariana was representing her. Her father had disappeared off the scene years ago and her mum was in and out of Mental Health Units. At present she was living with her maternal grandmother since her mother was in hospital again. However, her gran, Mrs. Green, had been diagnosed with a progressive muscle wasting disease. The local Social Services Department was assessing whether an aunt and uncle might present a more stable long-term home. Jade and her granny were inseparable, and Jade did not want to move. Today the conversation started with updates about Mr. Perkins which somewhat broke the ice.

Fred Boggis had originally been appointed handyman in Titus Tethering's time as Managing Partner. It seems Fred, who was a man in about his sixties, had succeeded his father Bob Boggis as handyman. Except for Titus Tethering all the other partners wished Fred would retire. Bad tempered, slow and expensive Fred had nothing to commend him except he would come at short notice. On one past occasion when called upon to do some repairs to external woodwork the partners had been concerned that he could not be seen and was extremely quiet. He was eventually found sitting on a crate in the boiler-house with another crate in front of him upon which he had placed a handkerchief as a makeshift tablecloth, and also his sandwich box, thermos of tea and a puzzle book. Words had been exchanged but Fred had insisted it was just his tea-break.

"My Doreen insists I must have regular tea-breaks," he said.

"My Doreen," was frequently quoted whether it was in support of his needing breaks or on world politics. Expressions such as,

"My Doreen says if we had lost the Second World War, the world would be a different place," were often forthcoming when Fred held forth. Another example was,

"My Doreen says that the trouble with poor people is that they don't have any money."

Fred and presumably Doreen too really did not like people other than people cut from the same cloth as themselves so Fred would also say things such as,

"Doreen says the trouble with foreigners is they come from other countries," or,

"Doreen says we should only do things the way people have always done in this country," and after they had been on holiday to Spain,

"It was very hot, and Doreen and I didn't like the food because they kept giving us Spanish food." He kept mumbling about, "Foreign gooey muck," and that Doreen had said that as they were at the seaside, "there should be good old English fish and chips."

When Ariana reminded Fred about locking up and the security codes he responded,

"My Doreen says if people behaved themselves, we wouldn't need locks and alarms," which of course was true!

Ariana always had to grit her teeth when speaking to Fred and not say what she really thought of the views that he and Doreen shared.

Fred had a long list of minor repairs to carry out plus some decorating in Mr. Tethering's room. Although he grumbled, he was glad of the work. When the firm employed a double-glazing company to do some of the conservatory update, he had been a little worried. Today he was due to fix a dripping tap in the first-floor ladies' toilet, rehang the door to the stationery and supplies room to stop it sticking and do some work in Mr. Tethering's room.

Mr. Tethering retained a downstairs office at the firm. It was a large room with a window which opened to the front of the building. When the other partners had tentatively suggested that as he only came in for odd days he might move to a smaller office and make his room available to members of staff who were there more often he would have none of it. The office had some faux oak panelling to waist height on the wall behind his desk above which hung a very unsmiling portrait of Queen Victoria. Also, on display on a hook in the office was a Victorian policeman's truncheon of which Titus was very proud. However, no computer could be seen in his office. Titus would write out instructions long-hand and members of staff would then have to transcribe them.

Due to the fact that Titus Tethering tended to crash his chair back into the panelling in his office each time he sat down or got up, over the years the painted panelling had become chipped and scratched in a line behind the desk. It was this area that Fred was due to sand down and repaint.

Titus Tethering's office had an odd stale odour. Titus would not let anyone look in his desk drawers. They were kept locked up in his absence. When he visited the office, he would put his lunch box and any spare fruit from the garden in his desk drawer. It was fair to say he often forgot the items he placed in the desk drawer. Last time he visited he brought with him some apples from his garden and some fish paste and hardboiled egg sandwiches. That was just over a week ago and they were still there now.

Even before he started painting Fred decided to open the window. He started with the top light. By the time he had put some high gloss paint on the panelling the odour in the room was overwhelming, so Fred opened the main window a small amount.

Taz and Baz were not the brightest sparks. Each had spent time in a young offenders' institution. Each had been represented by *Spong, Salter and Tethering*. Neither lad seemed to learn that there are no easy answers in life. Both young men had a sense of grievance and a view that things should and would fall into their laps. It neither occurred to them that solicitors don't have much cash in their offices nor that robbing your own solicitors was not a very sound idea. Still, in between smoking joints and picking their spots they thought they would attempt a break in at the offices and see what they could get.

"Should be money and computers," said Taz.

"Yeah, them solicitors is all rich so they will have plenty of dosh and won't miss nothing," replied Baz. It had also not occurred to him how he would sell password protected legal hardware.

They had also not thought about transport or time of day, so they set out in the late afternoon on their bicycles for the road which contained the solicitors' offices, a few other small businesses such as accountants and a terrace of Edwardian town houses. In the house immediately opposite *Spong, Salter and Tethering* lived the Khan family. Their front room faced outwards towards a small front garden, and they then had a view of the solicitors' offices opposite. Aziz Khan and his wife Amina were enjoying playing with their toddler twins while their older daughters Samira and Maya looked on. It was not often that they got time together as a family, so they were enjoying the otherwise quiet afternoon. When Aziz Khan was not managing a local plumbing supply company, he was often out doing his duty as a Special Constable. Amina's time was filled not only with caring for the family but also a part-time position at the post office counter.

While the Khan family were enjoying some family time Davy was eating pizza at a local branch of a chain restaurant *Fab Pizza.co* and was not finding the food that 'fab'. He had a doughy slab of something topped with stringy indigestible cheese and something mysterious which came in orange lumps and tasted disgusting. He did enjoy the company and when he came out of the restaurant he chatted to an amiable young trainee called Amelia. She had come on the bus and if she missed the next bus, she would have a three-hour wait. Although a handful of the trainees talked of going to the pub it was plain that Amelia was worried about her bus. Davy and Amelia agreed they would meet after work one day and go to the cinema. He had recently passed his driving test so he would try and borrow his mum's car.

As Davy and Amelia stood outside *Fab.Pizza.co* in the dusk light saying their "goodbyes" to each other and the other trainees, Davy was aware of grumbles and lurches from his stomach in protest against the recent pizza. He did not want to embarrass himself in front of Amelia, so he did not want to bolt back into the pizza restaurant. Fortunately, he was quite close to the office. As soon as she started heading for her bus Davy walked briskly to the office. He could see the light on in Mr. Tethering's office and was aware Fred Boggis was working at the office that day, so he just tried the front door and did not even need his key. He hurried inside and disappeared into the Gentlemen's toilets.

It was just about dark when Taz and Baz arrived. It did not occur to them that a light on in the office meant someone was in the offices. It did not occur to them to try the front door. They spotted the open window at the front of the offices with the light on in the room. At that moment Fred Boggis was just tidying up and had gone to fetch tools he had left around the offices and a bag he left in reception with a view to locking up and going home. He was no more aware of Davy in the Gents' than he was of the arrival of the burglars.

Taz and Baz each pulled their baseball caps down and tied scarves around their mouths.

"We should look the part, bro'," said Taz as his bicycle fell over with a clang drawing the attention of Mr. Khan to the scene opposite.

Baz climbed through the open window immediately followed by Taz. Just as Taz landed in the office Fred Boggis returned to the room.

"Who the hell are you?" he yelled.

"Why are you here?" shouted Baz seizing the old, policeman's truncheon from its hook and brandishing it.

Fred picked up the nearest item he could grab in response, but this turned out to be a paintbrush. Baz brought down the truncheon on the brush which fell to the floor and Fred retreated hastily. He dashed out of Mr. Tethering's office, and along the corridor which led to the conservatory. There was nowhere else to go except into the conservatory. Quickly undoing the yale lock and letting himself in, he was not quick enough to shut the door behind him, nor did he know the location of the key for the outer door to the car park since it had been carefully hidden inside a book on the shelves. He ended up with his back against the outer conservatory door with Baz about to lay into him with the old truncheon.

Suddenly, as if from nowhere, but in reality, from the shelf, Mr. Perkins leaped onto Baz's face with a hideous yowl. Baz dropped the truncheon and it clattered to the floor.

"Get him off, get him off," yelled Baz.

Taz made to grab the truncheon from the floor, but he was pushed back. Davy Dines had been washing his hands in the Gents' and feeling somewhat recovered from the appalling pizza, when he heard a commotion. He had emerged from the Gents' to see Fred pursued up the corridor and now he came to Fred's aid with the intruders.

Mr. Perkins stuck fast to Baz's face yowling with Baz screaming. There was pushing and shoving between Taz and Davy and Fred as well. A voice suddenly called out,

"This is Special Constable Aziz Khan; I am placing you two intruders under arrest on suspicion of burglary. Reinforcements are on the way."

Mr. Khan had seen the burglars climb through the window. He was vaguely aware Fred was working in the office and recognised him as a regular visitor to the premises having occasionally tried to pass the time of day with him without much success. He was also used to seeing Davy coming and going through the front door in recent times. He had come across the road and simply entered through the front door.

Taz stopped resisting and started crying.

Baz yelled, "Get that thing off my face, I'm the victim here."

Special Constable Khan attempted to grab Mr. Perkins, but Davy pulled him back,

"No, no, no, let me," he said and then to the cat, "Mr. Perkins, come on, you've done your job… come to me and I'll find you some nice food." He held his arms out and to everyone's amazement including himself, Mr. Perkins leaped into his arms and started purring.

"That thing should be put down," said Baz whose face had streaks of blood running down it from a number of scratches.

"No, that animal is a hero," said Fred Boggis who had been very quiet. "I reckon he saved me from them two criminals. I shall tell my Doreen to cook him a special meal of chicken…"

Mr. Perkins purred very loudly.

"And you, Davy, you're a hero too… and, Mr. Khan so are you… even though you're a foreigner."

Mr. Khan thought of protesting about the latter comment, but at that point back up arrived from the local police station and Baz and Taz were duly handcuffed.

Baz tried once again to protest about Mr. Perkins but was met with a chorus of indignation from Fred, Davy and Mr. Khan who said to the police officers who were in the course of leading the burglars away,

"Take no notice, I think the office pet just got caught up in the melee."

At that moment Ariana Twycross arrived, having been summonsed as a key-holder. Davy and Fred briefly told her what had happened.

"That cat's a hero," repeated Fred.

Ariana hastily went to the kitchen and opened a sachet of *Empress Delicate Morsels* which she decanted onto a saucer. She speedily returned and Davy put Mr. Perkins down who wolfed down the food and purred contently.

"You saved the day," she said as he climbed back on the shelf and curled up. Meanwhile the humans had to take care of the aftermath of the failed burglary.

Chapter 6

Ariana Twycross

A riana Twycross spent so much time being good to other people she never made time for herself.

As a child she would be the first to run over to a classmate if they fell over and grazed a knee. She would volunteer to clean the teacher's desk and to pick up litter from the playground. At home she was known in the family as a good and charming child. She would rescue wild creatures such as hedgehogs and take them to a local wildlife sanctuary. For a period of about two years, she had a raven with a broken wing called Roger, who she single-handedly nurtured. It was assumed that she would grow up to be a doctor or a nurse or a veterinary surgeon. However, Ariana had no aptitude for science whatsoever and also had a tendency to feel faint at the sight of blood.

She therefore announced to her family when she was a teenager,

"I will be a lawyer and help people who don't have happy families like mine."

So she went to university to study law and in due course qualified as a solicitor.

When she was at university, she met Salvador d'en Castell who was on a scholarship to study physics and artificial intelligence. Coming from Catalunya and speaking Spanish and Catalan as well as Italian and French, English was just one of many languages he spoke. Salvador was something of a genius and had been snapped up by an English IT company on his graduation. He was a little shorter than Ariana, swarthy and far from handsome. He had a very slight nervous tick. Ariana had spotted him looking nervous and worried in the university canteen. Initially she befriended him as she would any person or creature in need, but something about him clicked with her. As for Salvador he could not help but become besotted.

Ariana and Salvador became inseparable and continued to live together after graduation. Ariana went to Spain and met his parents. Recently, despite the fact they had been engaged for ten years she had not visited Spain for many years. Only his mother now survived who he visited twice a year without Ariana. His siblings and wider family seemed like shadows in the distance as he hardly saw anything of them. The wedding never seemed to happen because Ariana was always knee deep in cases helping people.

They did not live far from the office in a messy Victorian semi with an unkempt garden. Salvador had a large room upstairs which he used for his IT research and Ariana had a small home office. Otherwise, there was a living room and a kitchen-diner downstairs, and upstairs their bedroom, a spare room, and a bathroom. They had a beautiful one-eyed white cat called Minnie, a pair of rescued parakeets Merry and Jelly, and a pair of rescued house rabbits, Andy and Pandy. It was a happy home yet somehow there appeared to be something missing.

Salvador had begged Ariana many times to proceed with the wedding and also to go with him and visit his mother.

"She is not getting any younger," he said. "She longs for us to make her a grandchild."

Ariana would sigh and sometimes pull a face and say something like,

"I just need a few months longer to finish my current caseload."

But after a few months there would be more cases.

Friends had urged Salvador to issue an ultimatum, but such were his feelings about Ariana he could not bear the thought of parting with her.

Ariana had few living relatives. Her one brother had emigrated to Australia where he lived happily with a wife and children. He had never returned to the UK, but Ariana and her brother had monthly video calls. Her mother had died soon after she graduated. Her father had dementia and lived in a care home where she visited him fortnightly even though he had forgotten who she was. Her grandparents were deceased. She had an auntie and cousins who lived in northern Scotland whom she never saw. Ariana kept in touch with her contemporaries on social media but rarely went to see them. However, such was the radiance of her personality no-one ever had a bad word to say about her.

Ariana was loved by all her clients and widely admired by other lawyers. She always remembered to ask after family members of staff. For special occasions she could be relied upon to bring in cakes or biscuits or even wine to the office. Sometimes she would go an extra mile to even provide a birthday or Christmas gift for a child in a case.

This year she had spent time on many complex family cases. There was the case of the ten-year-old disabled child with the unfortunate name of Heaven Evans whose parents loved her dearly but could not abide each other. Little Heaven had limb deformities which needed multiple operations. Her parents Eva Evans and Evan Edgar Evans would use every type of insult for each other, occasionally in front of Heaven and had been known to strike each other with kitchen implements.

The court had appointed a children's guardian, Stella Patience, who had years of social work experience to represent young Heaven and she in turn instructed Ariana. Ariana made it her business to get to know her clients however young. Since Heaven spent half the week with each parent Stella and Ariana decided to see Heaven after school away from either parent using the office conservatory and with Mr. Perkins in attendance.

He sat on Heaven's lap and purred loudly while Stella and Ariana chatted to Heaven. After they had talked about school and what she liked doing and explained the court process in child friendly terms, Heaven said,

"Can I tell Mr. Perkins a secret?"

"Of course you can," they both replied.

"Mr. Perkins," she said, tickling him under the chin with the grown-ups listening, "I would like to go and live with my granny who has cats on a farm and just see Mum and Dad some weekends to check they are okay. I would not have to hear them argue when one of them fetched me or hear them say nasty things about each other to me… and I could play with Granny's cats who are nearly as nice as you."

"Miaow," said Mr. Perkins in apparent agreement.

Ariana had been involved in several very taxing court hearings in respect of Heaven and other children. One of them was Jade Green who at the age of fifteen was old enough to come to court. A compromise had been reached to Jade and her granny's satisfaction. Jade would live with her aunt and uncle in the week and have tea with her granny at least once a week. She would stay at her granny's house three weekends out of four but there would be flexibility about the arrangement.

Ariana had stayed late in the office to type up her notes with Mr. Perkins sitting at her side. Time was getting on and Salvador waited at home for her. She reached for another file.

Mr. Perkins jumped on her desk and sat in front of the keyboard and computer screen.

"Miaow," he said.

"Mr. Perkins please move out of the way," said Ariana. He moved to one side and then onto a shelf where she kept a picture of Salvador. He knocked it down and it tumbled into her lap.

"Miaow," he said.

She picked up the picture and looked at the image.

"Oh, Salvador," she said and attempted to put the picture back on the shelf only for Mr. Perkins to knock it back into her lap again.

"Okay, okay, I suppose it is late. I give in. I'll go home to Salvador," she said and stroked Mr. Perkins who purred loudly.

When she turned the key in the lock and entered her home, delicious aromas filled the air. Salvador was cooking. He called out cheerfully,

"By your standards you are early. I am cooking you a shellfish and fish stew. I have some nice wine chilling so for once you can sit down and I hope to have a lovely dinner."

"That sounds wonderful," said Ariana.

"How come you made it a bit earlier?" asked Salvador.

"Mr. Perkins," replied Ariana. "He kept knocking your picture down and somehow that encouraged me to stop and come home to you."

Salvador smiled, although he could not figure out how the cat had encouraged her to come home. They had a nice evening together. Later Salvador raised the issue of Christmas,

"I would really like to visit Mama and it would do you good to take a proper holiday."

"I don't know," said Ariana, but she didn't say 'No'.

The next few days at the office were very busy. The partners and staff still had to deal with the aftermath of the burglary. Statements had to be given to the police. Forms had to be filled in for the insurers. Fortunately, not much had been damaged. Inexplicably, Baz and Taz had asked for the firm to represent them. They were soon disabused of this notion.

Mr. Perkins did his rounds visiting his people in his usual fashion, spending quite some time with Ariana who was looking at some emails from a local charity which had connections with a local primary school. The school provided support animals to visit the school, in particular to encourage children with their reading.

"What do you think, Mr. Perkins? Can I take you to the school?" asked Ariana. Mr. Perkins purred in response. "I shall have to consult everyone else in the office. It would only be for a morning so hopefully it would be alright."

She bent down to stroke him and somehow dislodged some papers which had been gathering dust on a side table. At that moment Bernard came into her room.

"Hello, Mr. Perkins," he said.

"Don't I get a 'hello'?" said Ariana trying to pick up the papers which were old magazines and leaflets about Salvador's hometown.

Bernard bent to help her pick up the papers and saw the leaflets.

"Planning a holiday?" he enquired.

"Well… nothing definite at the moment," said Ariana.

Bernard responded, "You deserve some time off. If we are not on hols ourselves Katy and I would be glad to look after your pets, plus we would keep an eye on Mr. Perkins! Katy is mad keen on animals. I think Katy and I won't go away until the spring."

The conversation then turned to whether Ariana could take Mr. Perkins for a morning to the primary school. Bernard indicated he thought some children would benefit greatly from encouragement from Mr. Perkins, so he certainly agreed to this plan.

"What do you think, Mr. Perkins, will you let Ariana take you to school for a morning?" asked Bernard.

"Miaow," replied Mr. Perkins with his tail erect. "Miaow, miaow."

Ariana and Bernard laughed. They felt the other members of the firm would agree with the idea. Bernard said,

"Don't get me wrong and I don't want to pry, but I have often wondered why you didn't have children yourself. You are so good with children and young people."

Ariana said something noncommittal and got back to work. It was true she seemed to have a way with children. She had always put it down to her dedication to her job. Now she could not get an image out of her head of taking a small Ariana or Salvador by the hand.

"You look thoughtful," said Salvador when she got home.

Ariana did not say much except ask him some questions about when he had thought of the trip to his mother at Christmas.

"Are you thinking of coming too?" asked Salvador.

"Maybe," said Ariana. Salvador did not press things further, but suddenly later in the evening she asked,

"Do you like children?"

Salvador had been putting away some dishes and dropped a plate on the floor with a crash. As they were sweeping up Ariana deflected the conversation away from ideas of small Arianas and small Salvadors and told him of her idea of taking Mr. Perkins to the primary school.

"I wondered if you would come with me," she said. "You could bring Minnie."

Salvador looked disappointed but said he would join her.

For the next couple of working days Ariana was at court involved in a trial but when she returned to the office, Mr. Perkins announced himself with a loud, "Miaow," and came into her room with his tail sticking straight up. After she had spent a couple of hours working, he eventually lay in front of the keyboard obstructing her from using it.

"Oh, Mr. Perkins, I'm very busy," she said. "I will have to move you."

She gently moved him to the side table. He hissed slightly. After a few minutes a leaflet about Salvador's hometown landed in her lap.

"You are very persistent," Ariana said with a laugh. "If you were a human I would say you were telling me to go to Spain with Salvador at Christmas."

Mr. Perkins purred.

She looked at the leaflet and suddenly another one dropped in her lap. It was an out-of-date flyer advertising flights to Spain.

"Okay, okay," I get the message said Ariana.

She took the leaflet home.

"Right," she said to Salvador, "just to show I was serious about Christmas look what I've been looking at!"

"That's hopelessly out of date, if you really will go for Christmas when I visit Mama I will go online today."

"Yes," said Ariana and with conviction. "We should go for two weeks."

"What brought about this change of heart?" asked Salvador.

"Mr. Perkins," replied Ariana. Salvador thought she was joking and laughed.

Next morning at the office Mr. Perkins called on her.

"I am going to Spain at Christmas with Salvador."

"Miaow," replied Mr. Perkins.

Just as she was saying that someone else would feed him the phone rang from reception.

"Mr. Khan from opposite would like to see you," said Maureen. Ariana came downstairs followed by Mr. Perkins. Ariana, Mr. Khan and Mr. Perkins went into an interview room.

"Is it about the burglary?" she asked.

"No… it's personal." He looked a little embarrassed. He cleared his throat. "My daughter Samira is due to leave school soon and she is not sure what she wants to do. Would there be any possibility of her having a little work experience at your firm?"

Ariana smiled. "Well I can't say today but I'll definitely talk it over with Mr. Walden who generally deals with that sort of thing, but I think it is possible we may be able to help subject to her wanting to do it and checking things with her school."

Mr. Khan smiled. "No rush," he said. "Many thanks."

He looked at Mr. Perkins. "There is the remarkable animal. He ought to have an award or something."

"Miaow," said Mr. Perkins.

They made their way out of the interview room and said their "Goodbyes".

Mr. Perkins jumped up onto a coffee table and a pile of magazines went flying. Ariana picked most of them up off the floor but as for one magazine Mr. Perkins jumped on it and stood holding it down.

"Alright, I give up," said Ariana and at that point he seemed to flick it towards her with his paws. It was a lifestyle and fashion magazine. On the front page was the heading of a feature 'Brides in Spain'.

"Mr. Perkins, you are amazing!" said Ariana picking it up.

"Miaow," was the obvious reply.

Ariana found herself drawn to looking at the magazine. There was a discussion about Christmas weddings in various regions of Spain, including the one where Salvador's mother lived and some attractive photographs. Mr. Perkins rubbed himself against her purring loudly.

That evening when she went home, she said,

"Salvador, you know years ago you asked me to marry you and I said maybe 'later'; does that question still arise?"

Salvador gave her a broad smile.

"Of course it does," he said. "When did you have in mind?"

"At Christmas in Spain when we visit your mother," she replied.

Salvador gave a whoop of joy and then flung his arms around Ariana.

"What made you finally agree?" he asked.

"It was the Perkins' effect," she responded.

Salvador looked puzzled.

Ariana continued, "It is very strange; he has a remarkable effect on people's lives."

Salvador was bringing their cat Minnie to the primary school when Ariana was bringing Mr. Perkins.

"You will see the effect he has when you come to the school," said Ariana.

The subject then changed to planning their wedding. They even talked vaguely about having children.

Chapter 7

Mr. Perkins goes to school

The headmaster of St Servatius Primary School had no idea who St Servatius was when he took the job at the school or why it had achieved this name. Mr. Goodedge (nicknamed Mr. Good-egg by those who liked and Mr. Good-itch by those who did not like him) had no remarkable features about him at all. He could be said to make the average man look less than average. His classes could be rather dreary, but he did have a talent for administration and encouraging others to do well, be they children or teachers.

He eventually discovered that when the school had been founded the town was nothing more than a village surrounded by fields. The Victorians had knocked down the original building and built a schoolhouse which was now used as the school hall and had doubled up as a dining room until a temporary building had been added in the nineteen-sixties which was still in use. Indeed, buildings had been added in the nineteen-sixties and nineteen-nineties and now the school was surrounded by a housing estate.

Trevor Goodedge discovered that the school had been founded by a priest with a limp called Father Edgar in medieval times and there had been a plague of rats at the time spreading Bubonic plague from their fleas. The priest had the foresight to employ a cat who was a prodigious hunter of rodents and thus kept his school safe from the rats. The locals had named the school after a fourth century priest Servatius who became a saint. The name had been kept even after the dissolution of the monasteries and it survived the introduction of Protestantism and the Puritans.

Not only did it transpire that St Servatius was the patron saint of the city of Maastricht, but he was also the patron saint of foot and leg disorders, rheumatism, and protection against rats and mice. Mr. Goodedge was unable to ascertain the name of the cat who had assisted Father Edgar. All he could discover was that the cat was black and initially the locals were suspicious of him not least because of superstitions about black cats, but later a panel had been painted in the local church to commemorate Father Edgar and his black cat. It appears the cat came to be revered, and indeed the school badge had a tiny emblem of a cat on it. Sadly, the panel failed to survive at the local church since it was painted over by the Victorians.

When Mr. Goodedge heard of the use of dogs and other animals to encourage children in their reading, he became intrigued by the idea. His wife Jenny Goodedge was also a teacher. She taught home economics at the local secondary school, and she had also heard of such schemes and was keen to encourage other people.

Their children Chrissie and Chris were still studying at the local college and living at home. A discussion therefore took place at the Goodedge dining table after work and college about the possible benefits of such a scheme while the Goodedge pets, a yappy, scruffy, smelly Jack Russell called Strombo, and a pale green budgie called Bombon looked on.

The diners toyed with their food. While Jenny taught home economics her home cooking left a lot to be desired to the extent Mr. Goodedge voraciously ate school dinners and Chrissie and Chris were fat and pimply from the amount of chips they ate from the chippy near the college.

"No one hungry again?" asked Jenny as something very odd was placed on the table. After being married many years, she still had not realised her cooking was met with suspicion and dread.

"It's an experiment," she said smiling. "It's got some fish and nuts in it."

Trevor did not have the heart to tell her it looked like something which ought to be fed to Bombon.

"I had to eat with the other staff," he said, remembering her other experiments. There was one he recalled involving chicken, tinned peaches and broccoli which had turned brown.

"We ate at college," said Chrissie. Chris nodded in agreement,

"Oh dear," said Jenny. "I'll have to give the rest of it to Strombo."

The dog seemed to make himself scarce.

"He's such a good dog. He doesn't insist on table scraps," she added. She had no idea there was a hole in the hedge and that Strombo made frequent visits to the neighbours two doors down. He would sit outside their back door which when opened would produce a routine from him of sad eyes and sitting up and begging. The pensioner couple at that house could be relied on for digestive biscuits and custard creams.

"There is jelly for pudding," said Jenny smiling. No-one reminded her they were over the age of eight.

Trevor said, "There is this new local charity which is organising to bring well-behaved dogs and cats into school so that the children can read to them. I think some of my school children could benefit."

"Well, that counts out Strombo then," said Chris. They all laughed.

Strombo could now be heard to be barking loudly. He would be very likely to have jumped up on the kitchen windowsill to bark at the immediate neighbour's cat whom he hated. This was confirmed by the clatter of objects which could be heard falling off the windowsill, a frequent occurrence in the Goodedge household.

"No, I would not take Strombo," said Trevor. "I understand that the animals are known to be well-behaved. I hear one of the candidates is a cat who lives at the local solicitors' offices. He is a black cat just like Father Edgar's mythical cat of the stories about the school."

The family were intrigued. Mr. Goodedge told them what he knew of the history of St Servatius.

Trevor felt there were several children who might feel more confident if they were reading to a cat or a dog in private than in front of the class. The school had developed a comfy library reading area with bean bags for the children to sit on and it was here they might be ready to read to an animal. Trevor was particularly concerned about three children.

First, there was Starlight whose mother Starr took her ten-year-old daughter to modelling sessions as often as she could. They looked like clones of each other, silver-blonde, blue-eyed, slim and with lips like strawberries. Starr was employed by the council as a telephone advisor, but Trevor thought she probably needed advice herself. He doubted if there was a book in the house. Starr did not seem too concerned about Starlight's lack of literacy. Her emphasis was on hoping Starlight had a modelling career while still a child. She had apparently tried to be a model herself when in her teens. She said to teachers,

"I never got to be a model as I got pregnant, so I want 'er to 'ave a go... cos she's beautiful."

Starlight was a nice-looking child to be sure but there were plenty of other children just as good looking and some better looking too. Due to be eleven very shortly, Mr. Goodedge felt her literacy should be far better.

Then there was Maisie, a painfully shy child with a stammer. Small, skinny and mousy, Maisie seemed to want to melt away into corners. Also aged ten she seemed often to be sitting on her own at break-time. She was the only child of two older parents and apparently had no cousins in the area either. Her home was somewhat isolated, and her family kept to themselves.

Finally, there was Billy.

Billy's big brother Taz had recently been arrested for the failed burglary at the local solicitors' offices. Billy was the youngest of five brothers at just nine years old, and after his father left, his mother had formed a new relationship and produced three little girls. Taz was on remand and the eldest lad was serving a sentence for pushing drugs. The next boy following Taz had gone to live with his girlfriend's family. That left Ronnie who was twelve and went to secondary school, Billy and the three little girls living in the three-bedroomed semi with Billy's mum Tracey and his stepdad Andy. Billy's dad Malc lived in the area's one and only tower block with his girlfriend Maxi and their two toddlers, Billy's half sister and brother, Tina and Turner.

Tracey was only forty-two but looked twenty years older than her years. Once the children got to about eight, she largely left them to fend for themselves. Andy was always disappearing in his battered multi-coloured van allegedly to collect scrap metal. 'Big Malc' as Tracey's ex-husband was nicknamed had his new family and whatever nefarious activity could earn him a bit of money without the authorities knowing, since officially he was unemployed and "on disability" due to "back trouble". Anyone who really knew him knew that was a bit of an afront to people with genuine disabilities including back trouble. Big Malc was as tall as he was broad. He had a shock of unkempt red hair and a number of tattoos of knives and fire-breathing dragons on his arms and neck.

Billy had red hair and freckles, bandy legs, bony looking elbows and gave the impression he would benefit from a hot bath and a good meal. There were unlikely to be any books at home. Yet Trevor and the teachers thought that given the chance Billy could turn out to be quite bright.

Simon Hart-Worthington and Joe Gordon had found Flora to be an easy dog to train. Joe had become involved in the charity which proposed to bring pets to school since he knew what it was like to have difficulties. Simon and Joe agreed that Joe should bring Flora to school. Salvador d'en Castell was of course bringing Minnie to the school and Ariana Twycross was bringing Mr. Perkins to the school.

The day arrived and Joe, Ariana and Salvador arrived at the school about half past nine one morning. Flora had behaved impeccably en route as had Minnie. Initially Mr. Perkins went "Miaow," loudly when Ariana picked him up at the office. Then Ariana said to him as she stroked him, "We are going to see the children at the school just for the morning."

Mr. Perkins fixed her with an almost hypnotic gaze and began to purr.

Flora was on her lead and the two cats were in carrying cases when they were brought into the school. Joe, Salvador, Ariana and animals were shown into the reading area of the school library. Flora sat quietly at Joe's feet and Minnie and Mr. Perkins emerged from their carrying cases and sat on cushions on a low table. Both cats looked warily at the children.

About twenty children sat around while Mr. Goodedge introduced the people and the animals. The children were allowed to take turns stroking the animals before being sent back to class except for Billy, Maisie and Starlight. There were lots of "oohs" and "aahs" by the children who particularly admired Mr. Perkins. He began to purr loudly. There was some speculation by the children if Father Edgar's cat would have looked as fine as Mr. Perkins. Mr. Perkins seemed to purr very loudly at this suggestion.

Mr. Goodedge was pleased the three most troubling pupils were at school today.

"Now, children," he said to them, "I am going to give each of you a book and you can read it for about fifteen minutes to one of the animals. Us grown-ups won't stay in the room, but we'll come back in about fifteen minutes and perhaps you might swop animals then."

Maisie seemed to shrink into the bean bag she was sitting on. Billy shrugged his shoulders and Starlight put her hand up.

"Please, sir," she said. "They won't touch my hair will they? Mum won't like it if my hair gets messed up." Her hair had been styled into silver ringlets.

Mr. Goodedge smiled and sighed, "No your hair won't be touched. But look, come and take this book and sit with Minnie the cat." He passed to her a book called *Dinosaurs and the History of Flight*. She looked as if she was wrinkling her nose.

He handed a story book to Maisie which he suggested she read to

Flora called *Favourite Fairy and Folk Stories*. Finally, he handed Billy a book called *The Sheep who went Shopping*. Mr. Goodedge had chosen books from what he knew of the children's ages and reading abilities.

"You will have Mr. Perkins initially," said Mr. Goodedge to Billy.

Mr. Perkins gazed up with a knowing look.

The adults left the room. Maisie sat on her bean bag and Flora placed her head on Maisie's lap. She began reading, initially falteringly to Flora. Flora gazed into Maisie's eyes with rapt attention. Maisie seemed to gradually glow and smile as she continued.

Starlight and Billy each had a bean bag the other side of the room. Starlight sat with Minnie who sat very still while Starlight began reading. After about five minutes she stopped reading and said in a shrill voice,

"It's boring and I don't like it."

Billy had been sitting stroking Mr. Perkins who purred very loudly. He had not started to read the book he had been given to the cat. He said,

"At least you've got a book you probably haven't read before. I read *The Sheep who went Shopping* ages ago. "

"I bet you didn't," said Starlight pouting. "People say you're thick and can't read."

"I read in secret," said Billy. "What's your book?"

"Something about dinosaurs and flying… all nature and science… dead boring," she replied.

Mr. Perkins suddenly said, "Miaow," and jumped down knocking *The Sheep who went Shopping* to the floor. Then he went over to Starlight's bean bag and peered up at Minnie with a hard stare. Minnie got up suddenly causing the dinosaur book to fall to the floor.

"Miaow," said Mr. Perkins again and appeared to be chasing the books across the wooden floor. He flicked one and then the other with his paw and his nose. The sheep book came to rest at Starlight's feet. She picked it up. The dinosaur book came to rest against the side of Billy's bean bag. He picked it up.

Starlight examined *The Sheep who went Shopping,* and began reading it and Minnie settled back down beside her. She started giggling.

"Ooh... a sheep wearing a pink dress," she said to Minnie. "And she's got a red necklace."

Billy started to finger the dinosaur book. It was a book which tied in flying dinosaurs to the development of bats and birds. On its cover it said, 'suitable for children 10 plus'.

He started to read it very quietly to Mr. Perkins. Ten minutes later Mr. Goodedge peered into the room. He was surprised to see that Starlight and Billy had swopped books. The children did not seem to have heard his approach. Mr. Goodedge could see Maisie smiling as she read to Flora. He could hear the odd giggle from Starlight as she read to Minnie. He could hear Billy reading in fluent tones to Mr. Perkins who looked inscrutable. Mr. Goodedge gesticulated to the other adults who were in the corridor that they should move away for now. Mr. Perkins glanced at the doorway and appeared to give an inscrutable look as Mr. Goodedge backed out.

The visit by the animals to school was a great success and further visits were planned. In Maisie's case there was already a tiny improvement to her stammer, and she would now shyly borrow books from the school library whispering, "It would be nice if that dog visited again." She had even been seen shyly sharing her library books with other children.

In Starlight's case the teaching staff came to realise that it was better not to give her anything too serious, but she enjoyed any book where shopping and clothes were a subject, even if it was about sheep. The most important discovery was about Billy's abilities. He appeared to have hidden his abilities and had a genuine interest in wildlife and science. Mr. Goodedge got him chatting,

"Would you like to read more books about science and nature?" he asked.

"Yupp," said Billy, "but there ain't nuffink like that in my house."

Mr. Goodedge didn't correct his grammar.

"It's alright," said Mr. Goodedge, "there is plenty more here at school you can borrow. You can keep them in a locker here. I will make sure you can have them out when you stay for 'after school club'."

Billy gave a rare smile. "It would be nice to read them science books and books about animals."

Mr. Goodedge asked him, "What made you change books with Starlight?"

"It was that cat Mr. Perkins, he kind of swopped the books," replied Billy. "I think there's something special about him like Father Edgar's cat." He fingered the badge of the black cat on his school sweater. "I reckon we should do an art project, sir, doing pictures of special cats."

Mr. Goodedge did not argue with Billy. It was a good idea. His mind kept focusing on Mr. Perkins and his influence on Billy.

"I do like that cat," said Billy. "And I 'fink I like big animals like horses and cows too. When I grow up, I'd like to work at a zoo or a farm. Maybe I could be a vet or a zookeeper."

Mr. Goodedge thought about Mr. Perkins for a few seconds again.

He conjured up an image of an enigmatic black face with yellow eyes. It was coupled with thoughts that he should help Billy as much as he could.

Father Edgar

Chapter 8

Honorary Partner

All the partners and staff had noticed Mr. Perkins' involvement in the firm. When the partners had their regular meetings, it was usual for Mr. Perkins to sit himself down on one of the chairs at the boardroom table. Generally, he snoozed with a loud purring sound but now and again he appeared to want to join in the discussion. For example, when there was a discussion about whether the office should purchase its milk and other refreshments from the supermarket or obtain 'cash and carry' membership Mr. Perkins sat up and said "Miaow," when Graham said that the office should make sure it purchased enough cat food. When Simon raised the question of buying almond or oat milk for vegans Mr. Perkins hissed.

Bernard said, "Let's not go off at tangents. A cash and carry membership might save us money on loo rolls and cleaning materials too. Aside from basic tea, coffee, sugar, milk and cat food I don't see the firm can buy much else on the grocery side. People make their own arrangements for food for lunch…The conservatory is at least a good place to sit."

Mr. Tethering was present for once.

"I remember when we had a tea lady," he said in a quivery voice. "There was a big urn she brought round on a trolley with chocolate Bourbon biscuits. Lovely woman was Mrs. Jones…"

"Well times have changed," said Bernard. "Shall we move on?"

"Not for the better," said Mr. Tethering ignoring him. "She would sit in the kitchen at lunchtime and make sandwiches for people. Lovely sandwiches they were. You could order one for ten pence."

"Oh yes. What were they?" asked Simon intrigued.

"Ham sandwich or cheese sandwich, with or without pickle," came the reply.

"And what else?" Simon queried annoying some of the other partners who wanted to leave 'Memory Lane'.

"Nothing else," came Mr. Tethering's response. "Why should there have been anything else?…Mind you, fish paste is nice… well, I am sure Mrs. Jones could have done fish paste if someone asked her. She was a lovely woman as I said… I can recall there was a popular song *Me and Mrs. Jones*… Each time I hear it I think of Mrs. Jones… mind you…"

"Miaow," said Mr. Perkins when fish was mentioned.

"Come to think of it," Mr. Tethering continued, "Mrs. Jones made Christmas cake. She would bring in a lovely Christmas cake for everyone."

"Thank you, Titus, for the recollections. We must move on," said Bernard.

Conversation soon turned to new accounting software and Mr. Perkins went back to sleep. So, it appeared did Mr. Tethering. He was leaning forward over the boardroom table mouth agape, glasses sliding down his nose emitting rumbling noises.

There was one final item on the agenda. A local animal charity wanted to present Mr. Perkins with an animal bravery award since word of the burglary incident had got around. Further, the partners themselves wanted to show their appreciation of Mr. Perkins. The local paper wanted to photograph any presentation to Mr. Perkins from the animal charity.

Graham Walden said, "I think we should throw a party in honour of Mr. Perkins. The presentation could take place then in front of invited guests including the local press. We could do our own award too... it would be good publicity for the firm and a bit of fun."

Bernard replied, "What can we give Mr. Perkins?"

"A nice big fish or chicken breast!" laughed Graham.

"Miaow," commented Mr. Perkins licking his lips.

"How about making him honorary partner?" suggested Ariana. "Although we should get him a big fish too!"

Mr. Tethering suddenly woke up with a start and nearly fell off his chair.

"Partner, partner... who are you talking about? We don't need any more partners," he said. "Who knows what a new man might do to the firm. We don't want some big fish from outside taking over."

The idea was slowly explained to Mr. Tethering.

"Ah," said Mr. Tethering, "a party, how nice! I like parties especially Christmas parties. I like Christmas cake... Did I tell you about Mrs. Jones the tea-lady who made Christmas cake?"

The partners all agreed there was just enough time to organise the party before Christmas. It would be the day before Ariana flew off to Spain.

Ariana cleared her throat,

"I haven't told anyone, but Salvador and I are getting married at Christmas so if you don't mind I would like to also arrange some champagne for the party since there will be plenty to celebrate."

"Bravo," said everyone except Mr. Perkins who said, "Miaow," and Mr. Tethering who said,

"You are coming back?"

"Yes, of course I'm coming back," said Ariana. "Going back to Mr. Perkins, I suggest we have a good photograph taken and framed with the caption 'Honorary Partner' and make a formal thing of it at the party... obviously get some nice salmon or trout for Mr. Perkins too!"

"Miaow," said Mr. Perkins.

The rest of the partners thought the plan to make Mr. Perkins an honorary partner was a very good idea.

Graham Walden agreed to take the lead in organising the party. He agreed to liaise with the animal charities, the local press, and guests who the partners wished to invite in addition to staff and family members. He managed to get the ever-capable Maureen from reception to organise some of the catering funded by the firm. She in turn recruited Cora and Davy Dines. Ariana ordered champagne and smoked salmon and some gourmet cat food and a rainbow trout. The date was agreed with the animal award charity. Invitations went out to the local press, the animal reading support charity, representatives from dog and cat rescue charities, Mr. Khan and his family from opposite and Mr. Goodedge from the primary school and his family together with a handful of children nominated by the school.

It was only the day after the partners' meeting when Ariana was in reception that Mr. Perkins approached her with a very loud, "Miaow." Then he jumped onto one of the chairs and sat bolt upright.

"I should try to get a photograph," said Ariana to Maureen and fumbled for her camera.

"Stay still," she said to Mr. Perkins.

"Miaow," he replied and obliged. She took a photo. Then he jumped high onto the reception desk and sat staring with his yellow eyes.

"Hold the pose," she said and took another picture.

Then Mr. Perkins jumped down and made for the coffee table where he reclined enabling her to photograph him in a different position.

"I should be able to get a decent picture out of these," said Ariana.

"Miaow," said Mr. Perkins.

Maureen laughed and said to Ariana, "I reckon he knew you wanted a picture and was posing for you."

Cora, who was also on duty, agreed and said she would fetch him some cat treats. Mr. Perkins started purring.

The party was held midday on a Saturday shortly before Christmas. The furniture had been moved slightly in reception to accommodate a large Christmas tree. A smaller one had been placed in the conservatory. The boardroom was decked out with tinsel and the furniture had been re-arranged so that the board table had been pushed back against the wall. It now sported a Christmas tablecloth and fine dishes of food which were covered with film until they were ready to serve. On a side table there were bottles of champagne, a good red wine, orange juice, apple juice and a big bowl of blackberry, apple and ginger wine punch with glistening slices of apple floating on its surface. Someone had also decorated the legs of a low stool with tinsel and a small label reading 'Mr. Perkins' had been placed to one side of it. A Christmas napkin had been placed on it in the style of a tablecloth. On top of the napkin were two bowls. One bowl contained milk. In the other bowl was the rainbow trout.

Ariana had shown Mr. Perkins the fish during the preparations but urged that the door of the boardroom be kept closed until later in the proceedings. She had stroked him and whispered to him,

"You can have your fishy later."

Maureen asked, "Do you think he understands?"

Ariana smiled. "It would be nice to think so."

Invited guests began to assemble. It had been agreed that Flora the dog and Minnie the cat could also attend as well as the human beings.

Mary Walden came armed with a bag of animal treats including a nice dog chew for Flora. Joe Gordon looked smart in a new suit and smiled warmly when Flora was admired. Davy Dines shyly introduced his girlfriend Amelia to his colleagues and to Mr. Perkins.

"You are beautiful," she said to him and got a loud purr in response.

"He's a very special cat," said Davy.

Ariana and Salvador took the opportunity to show off Ariana's recently acquired engagement ring. It had a large yellow amber stone in its middle and was of antique silver.

"I chose it because it reminded me of Mr. Perkins' eyes," said Ariana.

"She could have had a diamond ring, but she preferred this one and dragged me into a little antique store when we were heading to the jewellers'," said Salvador.

"It was in the window and the shop was called *The Cat's Whiskers* so how could I resist?" said Ariana.

Mr. Perkins looked on enigmatically.

Mr. Khan and his wife Amina arrived with their daughters Samira and Maya and their toddlers in a double buggy.

"There is the hero cat," said Mr. Khan pointing to Mr. Perkins who purred loudly.

The toddlers cried out, "Nice pussy, nice pussy," and had to be restrained.

Bernard had brought his daughter Katy along and she soon recognised Maya since they were in the same class at school. The two young girls were soon busily engrossed in conversation interspersed with stroking Mr. Perkins.

Fred and Doreen Boggis were guests at the party. Without asking anyone, Fred gave Doreen a tour of the offices and they then returned to reception for a glass of wine. Doreen made embarrassing loud pronouncements on the décor and how she thought the furniture should be arranged. Ariana was showing Cora and Maureen her ring in reception. On seeing Ariana's ring and hearing of her imminent marriage she could not resist making pronouncements on this as well.

"You should have insisted on diamonds," she said loudly and embarrassingly, and then even worse she said, "you sure you want to go galivanting off with some Dago?"

Ariana looked so uncomfortable, and Salvador looked justifiably furious. Mr. Perkins apparently chose that moment to misjudge a jump onto a table and he sent a couple of glasses of wine flying, one of which scattered its contents over Doreen before falling tinkling on the floor.

"Ooo, I'm all wet," said Doreen which wasn't quite true.

Cora quickly intervened. "I best get a dustpan. I don't want glass in Mr. Perkins' paws. And shall I get you a cloth, Mrs. Boggis?"

Doreen seemed a little flustered and glowered at Cora who she appeared to dislike as well.

"I don't want any fuss," she said although that was probably not quite true.

Fred intervened. "I'll show you where the Ladies' is, dear, and then maybe we can go and sit near the buffet in the nice big boardroom."

"Yes, alright," responded Doreen.

Fred ushered her along a corridor muttering, "Try to keep your mouth shut. You're very embarrassing."

Doreen could be heard in reply, "You've never spoken to me like that before."

"First time for everything," muttered Fred.

Doreen was very quiet for the rest of the party.

Trevor and Jenny Goodedge not only brought their own children Chrissie and Chris to the party, but they also brought Billy to the party. They had very much taken Billy under their wing. For once looking well-scrubbed he was all smiles when he came into the offices, especially when he saw Mr. Perkins. Starr had not needed much persuasion to bring Starlight to the party since she had heard the press would be there and told Starlight,

"You try and get into the picture with that cat."

A little bit of persuasion by Trevor had persuaded her to pick up Maisie and bring her along with Starr.

Once the buffet was open Chris and Chrissie needed very little persuasion to partake and were soon happily munching delicious food in sharp contrast to their mother's dreadful cooking. Starlight dragged her mother by the hand to the place where Minnie was sitting.

"You're a nice pussy," she said.

"She's only got one eye," said her mother.

"That doesn't matter cos she helps people with their reading," responded Starlight and then she paused and said, "I like modelling, but when I grow up if I am not a model I'd like to help people or animals... maybe a nurse. At a hospital or a vets'."

There came a "Miaow," from Mr. Perkins who was nearby and being admired by Billy and the Goodedge family.

"One day I should like to see wild cats in Scotland," said Billy.

"One day I am sure you will," said Mr. Goodedge. Mr. Perkins seemed to purr in agreement.

Maisie sat and patted Flora and talked quietly to Joe and Simon about the books she was reading and Flora's favourite walks.

There was a further disturbance in reception when Mr. Tethering came in with his daughter Serena. Since the furniture had been moved Mr. Tethering seemed somehow to misjudge his route through reception and got his stick caught around a chair. The chair seemed to slew outwards, and Mr. Tethering fell into it.

"Ohh," he said, but was soon distracted by Mr. Perkins jumping into his lap and purring.

"Nice, puss, fine, puss... you caught the naughty burglars," said Mr. Tethering.

"I didn't think you liked animals?" said Serena.

"Well," said her father, "I do now."

"I've been saying for ages you should have a pet as company," persisted Serena.

"Well it wasn't the right time," old Mr. Tethering retorted.

Eventually Bernard Salter-Smith banged an old gavel down on the side of the reception desk.

"Ladies and gentlemen... and animals, can I call for quiet so we can proceed with presentations before we go on with the party?" he said.

"First, the Animal Heroics Trust would like to make a presentation to Mr. Perkins... could their representative and Mr. Perkins step forward?"

Mr. Brown from the Trust came forward with a rosette, a small silver cup with the words 'Perkins cat hero' engraved on it, and a packet of cat treats. Mr. Perkins obligingly sat himself up on the centre of the reception desk. The rosette was pinned to his collar with some difficulty. It was red and had the words '1st prize' in the middle. There was a flash of lights from the press camera and others also took pictures. Bernard accepted the cup on behalf of Mr. Perkins who was then offered some cat treats.

"Miaow," he said.

There was a slight hubbub, so Bernard cleared his throat and said,

"We are not quite finished so can we have a little quiet for a few more minutes?"

"Miaow," added Mr. Perkins. Everyone was quiet.

"First," said Bernard, "I wish to congratulate Ariana and Salvador on their forthcoming wedding. I am sure you will join me in wishing them every happiness."

There were cries of, "Hear, hear," and, "Cheers."

"Second, I want to say a well done to all three animals for their work at the primary school. This is an animal friendly firm so I want to encourage the various animal charities represented today and I think we should raise a toast to them and to Flora, Minnie, and Mr. Perkins... Cheers!"

A cry of, "Cheers," echoed around the room.

"Last but not least," said Bernard, "Mr. Perkins has been so remarkable the other partners and myself wish to make him an Honorary Partner... I don't think there are many cats who are partners of firms of solicitors..."

Ariana stepped forward with the framed photograph of Mr. Perkins with the label 'Honorary Partner'.

"This will hang on the wall in the boardroom in pride of place," she said.

The flashlights went again. Cries of, "Hear, hear", "Bravo" and "Cheers" could be heard.

Mr. Perkins said, "Miaow," very loudly and then jumped off the reception desk and towards the stairs.

"Where's he going?" queried Billy. The query was echoed by the other children.

"Don't worry," said Ariana, "I think I know."

Ariana led the children and Bernard upstairs to the boardroom, closely followed by Graham and Mary and by Simon. Most people had been in reception for the presentations, but Chris and Chrissie could be seen munching in a corner of the boardroom. Doreen Boggis sat on a chair looking thunderous on the other side of the room. Fred had left her there to view the presentations.

As for Mr. Perkins, he could now be seen at the specially decorated stool starting to tuck into his rainbow trout.

Chapter 9

Maureen and Cora

Maureen was polite but formidable, pleasant but firm and smart but under-stated. As the receptionist for *Spong, Salter and Tethering* it could be said she wielded a certain amount of power. She had been employed for about fifteen years on reception. Now in her early fifties she gave the impression she could rise to any challenge. It might be said that even some of the younger solicitors were in awe of Maureen.

Maureen had two cats at home, Mish and Mash, a pair of beautiful tortoiseshells. More was known about them than her husband Phil who apparently spent a good deal of time working away from home in oil rig engineering. Maureen and Phil had no children. However, also at home was Phil's mother Grace, and Maureen's mother Celia. By all accounts it seemed that the old ladies spent a good deal of time fighting so it was probably a relief to Maureen that she had a responsible full-time job. Sometimes, if Maureen had imbibed a sherry or a glass of wine or two, she would tell of the fights between the old ladies. It did not seem that Maureen had much time for herself since when she was not working, she was caring for her elderly lodgers. Now and then any precious days off were used to ferry the old ladies to any medical or other appointments. Additionally, she would find herself cleaning and polishing the house since Grace and Celia both complained about the standard of cleaning undertaken by the cleaner Maureen employed three days a week.

The main trouble with the old ladies was that they were opposites. Grace was loud, rather deaf, liked a brown ale if she could get it and enjoyed watching wrestling and boxing on television. Celia had been a teacher as a young woman and fancied herself as a poet. She was particularly partial to listening to the works of Mozart and Vivaldi and was teetotal except for Christmas and birthdays. It appeared that the two old ladies who were both eighty-two and thus approaching Titus Tethering in age, were company for each other but otherwise hated each other.

It also appeared that for whatever reason Celia's poems were about fruit and vegetables. She would endlessly boast about when her poem about asparagus was printed in the local paper, while Grace would make snide remarks about "people who get above themselves".

There was an armchair in Maureen's lounge which both old ladies regarded as their favourite. On one Saturday Grace got there first to watch the wrestling. Celia had wanted to watch the BBC symphony orchestra and told Grace in ringing tones,

"Where am I supposed to sit, on your lap?" She then proceeded to change the television channel. Grace threw her knitting at Celia and Celia responded with a copy of *The Times* crossword. Maureen had to intervene in this and similar incidents before the old ladies came to blows.

Sometimes Maureen would come home to be pounced on by either Grace or Celia with a litany of complaints about the other. Curiously when she got home, she would find them sitting together, sometimes comparing notes on some knitting or crocheting and sometimes doing the crossword puzzle together.

The cleaning lady would heat up a hot meal for Grace and Celia on Monday, Wednesday, and Friday. On Tuesday and Thursday Maureen would leave out sandwich and cake and if she had time would pop home for half an hour. The old ladies expected a full cooked Sunday lunch and Maureen found it very difficult to take them out to lunch when Phil was not at home. They were both mobile enough to walk in and out of restaurants and had good appetites. The problem was their constant bickering. This tended to reduce if they were occupied. For example, in the summer drives out to stately homes were more successful because Grace and Celia could be distracted by what they were seeing.

Maureen would sometimes admit that home did not feel like home anymore. She preferred to sit in the garden or even the greenhouse with Mish and Mash than sit with Grace and Celia. In the office she felt in her element, but at home she somehow felt an outsider. If the subject of the old ladies was raised, it was suggested to her by Simon Hart-Worthington and others she should look for care homes for them. Yet, Maureen felt that neither Grace nor Celia needed that level of care as yet however trying they might be. Indeed, they had recently been quite enthusiastic to 'help' with Christmas festivities. Grace had insisted on making a Christmas pudding and Celia had made some fancy table decorations. Christmas dinner had been relatively peaceful. Grace and Celia started arguing over Boxing Day television so at that point Maureen had slipped out and had spent a couple of hours feeding and fussing Mr. Perkins at the office.

Maureen did her best to take Cora under her wing. By all accounts Cora had not had the most auspicious start in life. Her mother, Truelove Smith, had been abandoned by Cora's father Christophe Henrici when she was born. Truelove had then discovered that Christophe had fathered six other children on five different islands of the West Indies. Truelove had then met Mark Mainard who had quickly married Truelove and given her three more children in rapid succession. Cora always referred to Mark as "father" or "dad" but not only was it clear he was not her father, but it was also clear he only tolerated Cora for Truelove's sake.

Mark Mainard was the proprietor of the local plumbing and heating supply company and Truelove helped in the office. When Cora was going to leave school and asked if there were any vacancies it was made abundantly clear that she was expected to make her own way in the world. Indeed, Mark encouraged Cora to leave school as soon as possible, ignoring any potential she might have to progress further through education.

Cora had suffered some degree of prejudice at school. It was not so much racism but the general nastiness of other young girls, since her year contained girls of many different backgrounds. In particular, her mother's first name provided a fair amount of sniggering. The fact that Cora was frequently top in English and History did her no favours with her classmates. Being "Cora Smith" the other girls made the association between apple cores and "Granny Smith" apples which only youngsters can and so Cora spent her schooldays putting up with the nicknames of "Apple-core" or "Granny".

Maureen found Cora was very quick at learning her job and did her best to make sure Cora was included in important events and tasks. Ostensibly to assist Cora with work she would take Cora out for a quick tea and cakes after work once a month before going back to the old ladies. While Cora was plainly fond of her mother and her younger siblings, they did not appear to have much in common. When Mark Mainard took the family for a quick week to the Spanish Costas or to Tenerife once she was aged over seventeen, she was not included, and Maureen got the impression she did not mind.

Cora appeared to have few friends outside work. She attended her local church and sang in the choir and was friendly with the minister's family. Indeed, she joined the minister's family for Christmas lunch.

Cora was very attentive to Mr. Perkins and her attention to him was reciprocated with loud purrs. She had a soft animal fur brush and on a quiet day between Christmas and New Year she was brushing him and talking to him.

"Did you know," she said, "the Latin for cat is *cattus* but the Latin for dog is *canis?*"

"Miaow," said Mr. Perkins.

"I didn't know you knew Latin," said Maureen to Cora.

"Well I only know bits," said Cora. "I was looking up some of the Latin phrases lawyers use like 'Habeas Corpus'... 'Corpus' means body, you know. So I guess it's to have someone or somebody. And 'Res judicator' means something has been judged I think. Then there is 'res ipsa loquitor'... means the thing itself speaks."

"All too clever for me," said Maureen.

Mr. Perkins said, "Miaow," and started wriggling. He dislodged a small display stand with leaflets from the local college of further education. Cora and Maureen started to pick them up. Maureen said,

"Look at this, Cora. This leaflet says they do courses such as Law A level in evening classes."

Cora looked interested.

Maureen said, "I reckon we should have a word with Mr. Walden at some point and see if the firm has any openings for you to train to do legal work since I think you are such a clever girl."

"I don't know," said Cora, but Mr. Perkins said, "Miaow."

Later, Graham Walden asked to see Maureen in his office. He had popped in for a few hours in the hopes he might catch Maureen.

"With all the Christmas celebrations I did not have a chance to tell you that I was hoping to give Mr. Khan's daughter Samira a chance of some work experience for a few days just after the New Year holiday. I believe you were aware in general terms of the intention to give her some work experience…?"

"That's right," said Maureen. "Miss Twycross mentioned she might spend some time on reception."

Graham continued,

"We have spoken to her. It seems Samira is thinking of a general office job after she sits her exams in May and June but meanwhile is after getting some experience. If it is okay with you I thought she might come in for a week in New Year week and spend it on reception, then another at February half term and then a fortnight in her Easter holiday. I have in mind that if we can accommodate another youngster and she is useful, then taking her on after her exams."

Maureen smiled and said, "We could always do with another pair of hands."

"I don't want to put Cora's nose out of joint," said Graham.

"Actually," said Maureen, "I was meaning to talk to you about Cora. The thing is she is really interested in the law… and very bright… but too embarrassed to ask if she could get involved in legal work."

"Thank you, Maureen," said Graham. "I will have a chat with Cora and also talk to the partners. I can't promise anything, but I will bear in mind what you say."

When Maureen came back to reception Cora asked, "What was that about?" Maureen just mentioned about Samira. Cora smiled. Mr. Perkins purred and looked enigmatic.

On a particularly frosty morning in the New Year, Mr. Perkins was lying by a radiator when Cora rushed into the office shivering. A few minutes later a sun-tanned Arianna invited her to her office for a chat. Mr. Perkins followed them into the room and sat at Cora's feet.

"Have you ever thought of training to be a lawyer?" asked Ariana.

"Miaow," said Mr. Perkins as if answering 'Yes' for Cora. Instead, Cora replied,

"I don't have a law degree and I need to earn a living… but in an ideal world I would love to be a lawyer."

Ariana said, "You know we have a couple of Legal Executives at this office… they didn't go to university."

"I thought Legal Executives were like solicitors?" said Cora.

"They are," said Ariana. "But their training is more on the job training. Someone can start as a school leaver and work towards some paralegal qualifications but then carry on becoming a Legal Executive. Over a number of years people can work to getting a degree. It can be a long route, but it's designed to fit round working life."

Cora looked interested and Mr. Perkins started purring.

"If you are really interested, the firm could help you start by qualifying as a Paralegal. If you were committed the firm could even pay for your courses and exams," said Ariana.

"I would love to do it," said Cora.

Ariana responded, "There will be a lot of hard work so I will tell you the websites to look at about the courses. Then I want you to spend a week shadowing Mr. Walden and a week shadowing me. You may be asked to do the odd task during that time. This will be in late February when for part of the time Maureen will have Samira on work experience. Is that alright?"

"Yes, of course and thank you," said Cora.

"Miaow," added Mr. Perkins.

"If at the end of the two-week period Mr. Walden and I, and of course yourself, all think it will be a good idea we will get you signed up for your training," said Ariana.

"I won't let you down. I'm thrilled to bits," said Cora.

Mr. Perkins just purred.

Cora told Maureen all about the proposal for her to train initially to be a Paralegal and then to be a Legal Executive.

"I am really pleased for you," said Maureen.

Cora said, "That's nice of you to say so but I hope someone can do something for you."

There was an enigmatic look on Mr. Perkins' face who was also present. He purred a lot and rubbed himself around Maureen's legs. He brushed against the coffee table in reception. The local paper fell down and some leaflets fell out of it. Maureen moved her bag to pick things up. She chided Mr. Perkins who just blinked.

When Maureen got home, Grace and Celia greeted her with various criticisms.

Celia said, "The fire has gone out. It's because you didn't clean the grate properly."

Grace added, "And you didn't leave enough wood in the basket."

"The house is hardly cold," said Maureen. "The central heating is on."

"But we're old," said Grace. And then she added, "And it's very boring here because SHE," pointing to Celia, "won't let me watch the sports' channels."

"Well, SHE," said Celia, "turns off my classical music... She's ignorant of culture..."

Maureen said, "Stop it, the both of you. I'll get my coat off and unpack the shopping and then see about the fire."

She took off her coat and hung it up and then started to unpack her bag. Some leaflets floated out.

"That cat must have knocked them into my bag," she muttered as the leaflets fluttered across the room. Grace and Celia picked them up. They appeared to be identical leaflets. They started reading them.

"Have you read this?" each asked Maureen.

"Why?" she retorted.

Grace replied, "It seems the council has just opened a new community centre in our neighbourhood. It even has a coffee shop. It has clubs for older people too. There's a bingo club starting for pensioners. I love bingo."

"How common," said Celia. "However, I notice that the pensioners' activities include a music appreciation society."

Maureen read one of the leaflets herself. It seemed the community centre was incorporating a pensioners' day centre with activities 10am to 4pm each weekday. There was even mention of a minibus staffed by volunteer drivers who might collect and deliver the pensioners. Separately some ladies were trying to set up a sewing and knitting circle on Saturday mornings.

"Shall we look into this?" asked Maureen. "It might be good for you both to get out of the house more."

Grace and Celia indicated agreement to her looking into matters. Celia said,

"But I will only attend cultured activities."

"Snooty cow," muttered Grace.

It took several phone calls and the local authority checking Grace and Celia were eligible to attend but Maureen managed to arrange for them to attend one day a week. The minibus would take and fetch them. They would eat lunch there. Grace could play bingo and Celia would be part of a group listening to classical music. Quite separately Grace and Celia managed to join the sewing and knitting circles. Although Maureen had to take and fetch them on Saturdays initially, after a while they made friends and were able to receive lifts. Somehow Grace and Celia became less acrimonious with each other. After some weeks Maureen found that not only had Grace and Celia become less argumentative with each other, but also she had Saturday mornings to herself.

One morning Maureen came into the office and was fussing Mr. Perkins when Graham Walden followed her indoors.

"You look very cheerful these days," he said.

"I suppose I am," she said. Mr. Perkins purred loudly as if in agreement.

"It must be the Perkins' effect," joked Graham before going to his office.

Mr. Perkins looked enigmatic.

Titus Tethering

Chapter 10
Titus Tethering

Although aged eighty-three Titus Tethering lived on his own in a five-bedroomed eighteenth-century house which stood in substantial gardens. It was a former vicarage in a tiny village which lay just fifteen minutes by car from the edge of town. The village boasted one shop and one pub and the church (although it had not had a resident vicar for fifty years). Titus still drove a car and he had two cars which he kept in the wooden garage at his property. One was a vintage *Morris Traveller* which was kept in good condition for him by a local car enthusiast and the other was an *Alfa Romeo* sports car from more recent times. Although some might have felt Titus' driving left something to be desired as far as he was concerned the odd scrapes were generally someone else's fault. After all, these large modern cars had large pesky wing-mirrors which tended to get in the way!

The substantial gardens to Titus' house included an orchard area, and the weeds were kept from taking over by local gardener Ron Storehouse. Although Ron had a face like a potato, he was a ladies' man and usually his current partner also acquired the role of Titus' cleaning lady. So far, he had had three cleaning ladies in seven years. He hoped Ron would settle with his latest amoure Brynne before his lifestyle gave him a heart attack and Titus had to get used to yet another cleaner.

Once 'The Vicarage' had been inhabited by Titus, his wife Joan, their daughter Serena, their son Gerald and various dogs and cats. Joan had died many years ago. Serena had become "something in the City". She had a penthouse Docklands' flat and a small flat in the next street to the offices of *Spong, Salter and Tethering*. She had never married nor shown any inclination to do so. Gerald had gone to work for a Wine Merchants. Eventually, on his travels to buy wine he had ended up buying a small vineyard in South Africa where he now lived. He was blissfully married to Chastity who had been living in an adjacent township and they now had five children. He worked the wine business as a co-operative with the locals. He had never returned to the UK and sent cards and photographs to Titus, often urging him to visit. The dogs and cats which had originally lived at The Vicarage had died years ago and had never been replaced.

Titus still enjoyed cultivating a few exotic plants in the Victorian lean-to conservatory at The Vicarage. He also enjoyed attending the fortnightly meeting of the local village gardening club.

Serena would have preferred her father had moved to a retirement flat some time ago and more recently had been muttering about care homes. Titus valued his independence although he did agree that these days The Vicarage seemed rather empty. He enjoyed his part-time working at his practice although recently the driving had become more of a strain. In his younger days he would enjoy looking into the more obscure cases and laws. One of his favourite cases involved the immigration status of a West African prince who had married the kennel maid from the local hunt. It transpired her father was actually a prominent member of the house of Lords so "daddy" was prepared to pay for a bucket-load of legal fees to secure a visa for her prince in this country. So successful was Titus that for a long time he kept getting invitations to watch the hunt return, followed by dinner, and also to polo matches. This in turn led to more immigration cases for fiancés of the country set who ranged from more African princes to South American tobacco planters' heirs.

In recent times the work was not so entertaining, but it was more interesting than sitting at home. Titus had also taken a liking to Mr. Perkins. He was now thinking about acquiring a cat or dog to keep him company. He had hoped that Serena might accompany him on a trip to South Africa, but she said she was far too busy. He had not travelled far in the last few years. His gardening club had organised trips to Kew Gardens and Chatsworth House, and a few years ago they had ventured across the Channel to visit the tulip fields in the Netherlands.

When he came into *Spong, Salter and Tethering* he always stopped and had a chat with Maureen at reception and these days he also made a fuss of Mr. Perkins. Not able to use computers or social media, Maureen was his source of news at the firm.

It was a frosty morning and initially Titus had to remove a layer of scarves and a hat before greeting Maureen,

"Brrr," he said. "The roads were quite nasty... glad to be here."

"Miaow," said Mr. Perkins.

"What's the news?" asked Titus Tethering.

Maureen replied, "Samira is getting some work experience with me today while Cora is shadowing Mr. Walden. Do you want a hot drink in a minute, I don't think Samira will mind making you one?"

"Any other news?" said Titus.

"I think you are fairly up to date. But there is one thing about which you might be able to help. A lady called Mrs. Beaudon from the local Refugee Society is calling in this morning on the off chance someone can help her. She rang first thing, and I was not sure we could help her, but she is coming anyway. The Society is assisting mainly East European refugees and she is not only looking for people interested in her work but also for some legal advice. She has an issue with the visa regulations for a few refugees coming to our town."

Titus Tethering smiled.

"Goodness me... I am a little rusty on my immigration law but maybe I could at least point her in the right direction. Let me know when she is here, and I will see her."

"Miaow," said Mr. Perkins.

Titus clattered his way with his stick into his office. It was quite spick and span after being redecorated by Fred Boggis. Samira brought him a cup of tea and Mr. Perkins ambled into his room before lying across his desk purring. Titus stroked him and said,

"You've never sat there before. Are you trying to tell me something?"

"Miaow," said Mr. Perkins with a knowing look in his eyes.

It was only about half an hour later that Maureen phoned through to say that Mrs. Beaudon had arrived.

"Please show her through," he said. "But check she is not allergic to cats as Mr. Perkins is sitting on my desk."

Maureen showed Mrs. Beaudon into his office having checked the position about Mr. Perkins.

"Do sit down," said Titus. "I hope you don't mind but the office cat has sat himself centrally."

"It's quite alright," said Mrs. Beaudon.

"I have to also warn you," said Titus, "I am a little rusty on immigration law and I am a bit hard of hearing these days… but if I can't help myself, I will do my best to point you to people who can help you. And I certainly won't charge you for today's visit."

Mrs. Beaudon smiled and said,

"Thank you. Any help is appreciated. We need help for some East European refugees… two families who have problems with visas and sponsorship and one teenage girl from East Africa who is in danger of being deported."

She went into more detail and Titus made copious notes with a fountain pen. Mr. Perkins purred loudly.

Titus said, "The East African girl. That's a completely different set of rules. I will get one of our trainees to see if there are any firms or organisations who have legal aid funding for her sort of case."

"Thank you," said Mrs. Beaudon. "It's not our normal type of case anyway. My main concern is about the visa and sponsorship arrangements for the two East European families. As a matter of fact, your cat reminds me that one is a mother and daughter who managed to rescue their cat and their dog, and they want to bring them with them. Do you want to see a picture?"

"Please," said Titus.

"Miaow," said Mr. Perkins.

"Their sponsor is not so sure about their pets. I don't know if that is holding things up," said Mrs. Beaudon.

She showed him a picture of an attractive young woman clutching a pretty little girl of about six who was cuddling a small brown dog and a tabby cat.

"Sadly her husband has been killed," said Mrs. Beaudon talking about the mother. "She is all on her own, stuck in temporary accommodation with the child and the pets near the border."

Mr. Perkins fixed Titus with a hypnotic gaze and he found himself saying,

"Could I sponsor them instead? I have a big house and a garden... there is loads of room... There is just me there."

Mrs. Beaudon smiled. This was better than she could have hoped. Mr. Perkins seemed to smile too. He purred very loudly.

Over the next few weeks Titus not only galvanised into action to get the refugee family and their pets into the country to live with him but he took the decision to retire from the firm to help with the work of the Refugee Society. By late April with his help his shy and traumatised refugee family arrived with their pets.

Something within Titus meant that he knew to give them space. Yet he derived pleasure from the mother's and daughter's smiles as the leaves slowly came out in his garden and watching their animals sniff about his flowerbeds.

His daughter Serena tried three or four times to dissuade him from looking after the little family. Finally, he said to her,

"You will always be my daughter, but you and I are different people. I have come to realise it's important to have people and pets around one. Maybe it would do you good to get a cat."

Serena seemed chastened. Titus' son Gerald sent him a 'Good luck' message from South Africa.

There was a buzz about the firm of *Spong, Salter and Tethering*, and as Easter came and went Ariana had a smile on her face and a certain glow about her. Soon Salvador and Ariana would be expecting an addition to their family.

Bernard had also allowed Katy to acquire a pair of kittens now that the dust had settled from his marriage breakdown. Katy was thrilled to allow Castor and Pollux into their lives. The lady who owned the kittens was also looking for a home for their siblings Alpha and Omega.

"Couldn't you have them at the office?" asked Katy.

"I don't know," said Bernard. "I'm not sure how that would fit in with Mr. Perkins."

There had been discussions around the office. A decision was taken to give a trial of having the further cats. Graham Walden said,

"Animals can be very therapeutic so if we don't try to see how it goes, we will not know."

The staff and partners of *Spong, Salter and Tethering* and those connected to them seemed to have a zest for life.

It was early May. It was a glorious day. Today was the day the kittens would arrive on a trial basis. Today was also the day of Titus Tethering's retirement party. It was also one year since Mr. Perkins arrived at *Spong, Salter and Tethering*.

It was late afternoon after the business of the day had been completed. A buffet had once again been laid out in the boardroom and there were bottles of wine, champagne and chilled lemonade. In the centre of the table was a large cake bearing the words 'Good luck Titus'.

As well as the staff and partners of the firm and their families and close friends, a handful of other invited guests had arrived. They included the Khans from opposite and the Goodedge family who had Billy with them. Billy seemed to be thriving.

Mary Walden was engaged in conversation with Simon Hart-Worthington and also Joe Gordon who had brought Flora with him. Katy had taken the basket with the two kittens through to the conservatory where Samira, Maya and Davy Dines and his girlfriend Amelia were admiring them.

Titus was sitting in his old office with his little refugee family and Serena where he was musing about the past and the future.

"It will seem odd to only come here as an occasional visitor," he said. "But I have the three of you."

Serena seemed to have reluctantly accepted the situation and was smiling.

Bernard Salter-Smith and Graham Walden were enjoying a glass of wine with Salvador and Ariana (who had lemonade) in the boardroom.

Bernard said, "There have been many changes this year at *Spong, Salter and Tethering* but whatever the outside world might sling at us I think the changes here have been good ones."

Graham Walden said, "We are incredibly lucky." The four of them all agreed.

Downstairs in reception Cora noticed something on the floor and called over to Maureen,

"Look, Mr. Perkins' collar has come off."

"Never mind," said Maureen, "I am sure we can put it back on him."

"Where is he?" queried Cora.

"I think he just stepped outside," said Maureen. "I am sure he will be back soon. Shall we go and see the kittens?"

They headed to the conservatory.

The black cat sat just outside the solicitors' office sniffing the sunlit air. He sat in a patch of sunshine on the pavement, his tail swishing as if in indecision. He turned his head and looked into the doorway with an almost longing look in his yellow eyes. The building cast deep shadows onto the pavement. When the black cat got up, he moved into the shadows. The dark form of the cat seemed to merge with the deep black shadows.

Mr. Perkins' Afterword
Of Lawyers and of Cats

There are about 11.1 million pet cats in the United Kingdom according to the People's Dispensary for Sick Animals (PDSA) in 2022, and in September 2022 the Solicitors' Regulation Authority (SRA) which regulates solicitors in England and Wales tells us that there were 219,932 solicitors and 9721 firms. No statistics are given on whether any firms had a pet cat on the premises.

England and Wales has a split legal profession. There are solicitors, barristers and legal executives. A qualified lawyer in England and Wales is someone who has a legal professional qualification which allows them to practise in the UK or an international jurisdiction. The Solicitors' Regulation Authority is the regulatory body which keeps the register of solicitors, and this register is the definitive impartial source of information about the law firms and people regulated by the Solicitors' Regulation Authority.

John Barkers' solicitors give one of the best descriptions of the difference between barristers and solicitors. They say online:

"A barrister is a legal professional who specialises in courtroom advocacy and litigation. Whereas solicitors usually conduct transactional work at the request of a client, a barrister will rarely be instructed directly by a client instead they will be briefed by a solicitor."

As for solicitors they say online:

"A **solicitor** is a registered legal practitioner who deals in the general aspects of giving legal advice and conducting legal proceedings for individuals and businesses. In order to become a solicitor a person must obtain legally recognised qualifications and obtain a practice certificate."

Barristers tend to work in Chambers whereas solicitors tend to work in firms. Barristers derived their name from being 'Called to the Bar', being the bar of the court where only certain people could appear as advocates before the judge. It used to be the case that only barristers could appear in the higher courts but nowadays solicitors can become qualified to do some higher court work. Also, certain barristers will now do some work taking direct instructions from their clients. The Bar Council is the professional body for barristers.

There are also legal executives who can work in law firms. Their training tends to be vocational, on the job but a chartered legal executive can in due course qualify to be a solicitor.

As the Law Society itself says:

"The Law Society is the independent professional body for solicitors in England and Wales."

Legal executives tend to be represented by CILEX which says of itself:

"CILEX is the professional association and governing body for over 21,000 Chartered Legal Executive Lawyers, other legal practitioners and paralegals."

Domestic cats are small carnivorous mammals. They are genetically related to larger cats. Although the origin of the domesticated cat is hidden in history it seems there were two possible lines of ancestry. One lineage appeared in the Middle East possibly as early as 10,000 years ago and travelled northward and westward into Europe. The other lineage appeared in Egypt sometime from a similar period spreading throughout the Mediterranean. Cats of both lineages continued to breed with the African wild cat. It seems that the ancient Chinese also domesticated cats including the leopard cat.

The ancient Egyptians revered cats to the extent they worshipped a feline goddess named Bastet, who was depicted as half-feline and half-woman. It is thought that rather than being 'tamed' cats were attracted by human activity, for example there would have been rodents around grain stores. It may be that the toleration turned to encouragement when the benefits of having cats around were noted. It is further likely that humans would have encouraged the friendliest cats. Most 'domestic' cats retain habits and instincts of their wilder cousins such as the wish to hunt small prey.

The European medieval world's association with cats was rather schizophrenic. Cats were to some extent demonised and associated with Satan owing to the medieval Church associating them with earlier pagan religions such as those of Egypt and Rome. Some villages were reported to have massacred cats. Pope Gregory IX issued a papal bull against cats especially black ones. It had unfortunate consequences for women who befriended cats as they were condemned as witches.

Yet on the other hand the cat became valued for its ability to deal with pests. This was particularly the case when there were outbreaks of bubonic plague in thirteenth century Europe. Although medieval man mainly ascribed plague to punishment for sin, when times were hard, he valued having his grain store protected.

The Protestant Reformation affected some of the beliefs relating to cats beneficially, yet there continued to be outbreaks of superstition ascribing evil to cats.

For a detailed account it is worth reading www.worldhistory.org which has a detailed article by Joshua J. Mark called *Cats in the Middle Ages*. For confirmation that St Servatius was known to be the patron saint against rats and mice the Dominicans give some information about him on www.willingshepherds.org. How he kept the rats and mice away is not made clear.

By the eighteenth century cats were kept as pets by several literary figures since keeping cats as pets was quite common. Dr Samuel Johnson had a cat who was apparently called Hodge and for whom he purchased oysters. The philosopher Jeremy Bentham who according to the St Neots Museum and other resources kept a cat who was called **the Reverend Sir John Langbourne**, and who ate macaroni noodles at the table, and who Bentham described as 'a universal nuisance'. The subject of Dr Johnson's cat and also Jeremy Bentham's cat would make a long account all on its own.

Horace Walpole writer and Whig politician had a cat made famous by her sad death. She apparently drowned in a goldfish bowl in 1747 and was made famous by a poem entitled *Ode on the Death of a Favourite Cat Drowned in a Tub of Goldfishes*. This poem by Thomas Grey was later illustrated by William Blake.

By the nineteenth century cats were ever more popular. Although there were many circumstances where cats were starved or ill-treated, people were encouraged by the notion that cats were by then regarded as clean and Godly creatures. Queen Victoria kept pet cats. She was reputed to favour Persian cats. The Royal Collection Trust has a painting of three of Queen Victoria's dogs and a kitten in a picture by Charles Burton Barber (1845-94) entitled *Cat and Dogs belonging to Queen Victoria* signed and dated 1885.

By the latter part of the nineteenth century the first cat show had occurred. Further, Florence Nightingale was reputed to have kept some sixty cats. The issue of one of her cats came to more modern public attention when a letter written to a friend came up at auction. In that letter she asks her friend to look for a home for one of them called Mr. Bismarck (named after the German Chancellor). In the end she kept Mr. Bismarck, and his diet is said to have included rice-pudding. See www.express.co.uk and www.dailymail.co.uk and other similar articles.

There is no doubt the great and the good and the not so good are attracted to cats. Catherine the Great was said to have liked cats. Abraham Lincoln was said to be a cat lover. Newsweek has a detailed history of which US presidents kept cats. See https://www.newsweek.com. President Clinton's cat Socks was probably amongst the best known.

Cats have been known for their residence on ships whether merchant ships, warships, or expeditionary ships. One such feline was Blackie, later renamed Churchill. He was resident mouser on HMS Prince of Wales and grew to fame when he met Winston Churchill in 1941 when Churchill had been going to a summit with Franklin D. Roosevelt and Churchill stopped to pet him.

Simon was the ship's cat aboard HMS Amethyst, a sloop which had served in the Atlantic during World War II, but he joined her in 1948. The ship was involved in the infamous Yangtze incident in 1949. When the People's Liberation Army fired on the ship Simon was severely injured. However, he seemed to make a full recovery and resumed ratting duties on the ship. He was later presented with the Dickin medal which is the animal equivalent of the Victoria Cross. Sadly, on the ship's return to the he died in quarantine, probably from infection to his wounds. See historycollection.com.

Ernest Shackleton's ill-fated expedition to the South Pole not only included several dogs, but a cat named Mrs. Chippy (actually a male). Mrs. Chippy's adventures are documented in *Mrs. Chippy's Last Expedition,* a book by Caroline Alexander ISBN 978-0-06-017546-7. The story is told from the cat's point of view .

From ships to grain stores to cosy places by the fire, cats are involved in all manner of activities. For example, in recent times the street cat Bob has been known for his good works and a statue has been erected to him (see *A Street Cat Named Bob,* by James Bowen ISBN 978-1444737110 and other books in the series).

As previously mentioned, Winston Churchill had lent his name to a cat. Churchill was a great cat lover. During his illustrious life he had a number of cats. There are several anecdotes worthy of mention.

One cat called Mickey was playing with the telephone cable when Churchill was on the phone to the Lord Chancellor. There was a brief misunderstanding when Churchill shouted at the cat, "Get off the line, you fool."

His best-known cat was a big grey cat called Nelson. He was reputed to have sneaked pieces of smoked salmon to Nelson during a dinner. Churchill did, however, express concerns over protocol at Downing Street as there was already a cat in residence who Churchill called the Munich Mouser.

Churchill's last cat was a ginger cat called Jock. When Churchill's residence at Chartwell was passed to the National Trust the family expressed a wish that there should always be a cat there called Jock. More can be read about Churchill and his cats on winstonchurchill.org.

The prime minister's residence at 10 Downing Street has had many cats in addition to the Munich Mouser. It is suggested that there are records in the National Archives going back to the nineteen twenties in respect of Downing Street cats. Probably the best recalled in modern history are Wilberforce from Edward Heath's time and Humphrey from Margaret Thatcher's era. Humphrey continued his tenure as 10 Downing Street cat in John Major's time but was then retired when the Blairs moved into 10 Downing Street.

Another well-known Downing Street cat was Sybil. In 2011 Larry took over as Chief Mouser to the Cabinet Office. He has had more longevity than most prime ministers. He is known to be a prodigious hunter of rodents and frequently catches the eye of news cameramen. For a while Larry was joined by Freya who was said to be friendly with George Osborne's family (former Chancellor of the Exchequer). Freya retired after one too many escapades with traffic. In 2016, Palmerston the foreign office cat joined Larry, but he too retired in 2020. Further cats have apparently been brought in to assist with mousing as has been explained in www.purr-n-fur.org.uk .

Cats are subjects of books, films and magazine programmes. From *Tom and Jerry* the animated television series by William Hanna and Joseph Barbera, through to *My Cat from Hell,* the American reality TV series fronted by Jackson Galaxy, cats are human beings' pets, irritations, companions and enigmas. In the UK Cats' Protection https://www.cats.org.uk is the largest feline welfare charity.

Despite the scrabbled-up gardens, the coughed up furballs and the dead rodents presented at the feet of our beds, cats give us a quiet companionship we cannot get from humans. They do not judge us (well… except as to the type of cat food) …and they do not pry (well… except where we are storing that nice chicken). Although tame creatures they retain a link with the wild. They are an enigma who deserve our respect.

Printed in Great Britain
by Amazon

17303408R00075